CLEAR ROUND FOR KATY

CLEAR ROUND
FOR KATY

by

DELPHINE I. RATCLIFF

LUTTERWORTH PRESS
GUILDFORD AND LONDON

The Publishers are grateful to Miss J. Kemp of Mounters Farm,
Chawton, Hampshire, for permission to take the cover photograph
at her riding stable

ISBN 0 7188 2255 2

PRINTED OFFSET LITHO AND BOUND IN GREAT BRITAIN
BY COX & WYMAN LTD
LONDON, FAKENHAM AND READING

Dedicated to
IAN AND ALISON

CONTENTS

CHAPTER ONE

A DISAPPOINTMENT

KATY sat on a bale of straw and gazed round the empty stable yard. She had hurried out of school, gulped down her tea, changed into an old pair of jeans and pedalled to the stables in record time.

"I thought Anne would be back by now!" she complained to a grey horse whose head hung over a stable door. "She cancelled all the rides to go to this sale, but I thought she'd be back for *my* evening lesson."

The grey horse's ears twitched back and forth, then he turned away to snuffle in his empty manger.

"I suppose I could muck out while I'm waiting. Anne would be pleased to find all the horses bedded down and fed when she gets back." Katy jumped up and went to find a fork and a wheelbarrow.

Just then a small boy with spectacles came cycling into the yard.

"Hullo, Clive," said Katy. "Anne's not back

yet—she's gone to a sale today. Didn't you know all the rides were cancelled?"

"No, I didn't," Clive replied, "but what's she gone to a sale for?"

"To buy a new horse, of course! I hope she's going to get a super show pony. She'll let me show it for her, I expect. Wouldn't that be marvellous."

"Why you?" asked Clive.

"Because I come here more than anyone else. I practically work here, you know. It's only silly old school that keeps me away. Anne is giving me special lessons in return for the work I do," Katy replied. "Oh, I do wish she would hurry up. I'm dying to see the beautiful new pony she's bought. Now—want to help me muck out?"

"Might as well," said Clive grudgingly. "There's nothing else to do."

There were only three loose-boxes to be mucked out and three horses to be fed, as the other ponies were turned out to grass. Clive and Katy were so engrossed in their task that at first they did not hear the Land-Rover and trailer drive into the yard. But they heard the ramp drop with a clatter, and rushed out to see.

"Hullo, Anne. Gosh, I can't wait to see what you've bought," Katy gasped excitedly.

"Steady now," said Anne, putting a finger to her lips, "he's a wee bit nervous—stand back and keep quiet while I get him out."

Anne climbed in through the groom's door and began to back the animal down the ramp. Katy and Clive stood by expectantly.

The first thing to appear was a straggly, black tail, then came a pair of rather large, hairy heels. The rest of the horse came out with a rush, Anne slithering down the ramp after him, hanging grimly on to the halter rope.

"There, what do you think of him?" Anne asked, leading the gaunt, brown horse round the yard.

Katy tried to conceal her disappointment. "Well, he's big, isn't he? I thought you were going to buy a show pony."

"The good ponies were making an awful lot of money today, Katy. I just couldn't afford any of them. I almost came home without buying anything, but then I saw Bracken. He looked so sad, and everyone who looked at him remarked on his Roman nose and thick hindlegs," Anne explained. "I felt sorry for him. I think he's been ill-treated, he's very nervous of strangers, and he's head-shy."

"What does that mean?" asked Clive.

"It means he is difficult to bridle, because he's nervous of anyone touching his head. Probably someone has hit the poor old boy round the head at some time or another," Anne replied. "Anyway, I decided to try him, and I found he was so quiet to ride that I made up my mind to bid for him.

We badly need a quiet horse for adult beginners. I got him very cheaply. So here he is—Bracken. Put some straw in one of the empty stables. We'll keep him in for a day or two, until he gets used to us."

So the new horse was bedded down and fed. Clive and Katy stood staring at him over the stable door while Anne went to put the trailer away.

"Gosh!" said Katy after they had contemplated him silently for some time. "Whatever made Anne buy an ugly beast like that?"

"She told you," Clive replied. "Because he's quiet enough for beginners, and she felt sorry for him."

Bracken paced restlessly round his stable, snatching mouthfuls of food from the manger and then going to the window to look out across the fields behind the stables.

Clive called to him and held out his hand, but Bracken regarded him suspiciously and wouldn't come near.

"Come on," said Katy, "leave the stupid thing by himself. I'm going to find Anne to ask if I can have my lesson."

Anne said, "Well, I hate to disappoint you, Katy, but I haven't eaten for hours. I simply must go in and have a meal. Tell you what, though, as you've both worked so hard—saddle up Whiskey and Biscuit and have an hour down in the schooling paddock. I'll come down when I'm ready, just to put you through your paces."

"Thanks very much," said Clive. "Come on, Katy. I bags Whiskey."

"Okay," Katy replied, "I don't care which I ride. Don't worry, Anne, we won't fool about. We'll do some serious schooling just as if you were there."

"You'd better," said Anne. "I'm putting you on trust. You know I never let anyone ride un-supervised as a rule."

Katy and Clive ran off to the tack room. The saddles and bridles hung in neat rows with the name of the pony to which each belonged neatly printed above every rack. They collected Whiskey's and Biscuit's tack and went to saddle their mounts.

Whiskey was a general favourite at the stables. He was a smart little piebald with perfect manners, safe for any child to ride. Biscuit was a dun, rather bigger than the other pony. Anne had not had him very long, and was having to give him a lot of schooling, as he could be a little naughty at times.

Katy and Clive were soon mounted and riding down to the paddock.

"Now," said Katy, "follow me round the track to start with, then when they've settled down we'll go opposite ways."

Clive was quite content to let Katy take charge, and he did his best to carry out her instructions.

She called out commands in what she thought was a very professional manner, but she hadn't a lot of patience and when Clive made an occasional mistake she would shout: "Not like that, you silly idiot."

Clive just muttered "Bossyboots!" under his breath and wished that Anne would hurry up.

They were both concentrating so hard on their riding, that Anne was able to watch them for a few minutes before they noticed that she had arrived.

"You are both doing very well," she said at last. "Katy, you have got Biscuit nicely under control now, and Clive, your sitting trot has improved enormously. Now, you can both have a nice canter round a couple of times and then we must go in, because it looks very much as if it is going to rain and none of us has a jacket on."

"Oh, bother!" said Katy. "I wanted to do some jumping when you got here."

"Can't be helped," Anne replied. "I'm not getting wet for you or anyone else. How I wish I could afford an indoor school, so that we could ride in all weathers. Still, it's no use wishing, I shall never make enough money for that. Hurry up now—the rain is starting. Twice round at a collected canter, and then *walk* them back to the stables."

Clive and Katy unsaddled the ponies and turned them out in the field with the others. Anne lent them a couple of old raincoats that hung in the saddleroom, and they helped to sweep up the yard.

They filled the water buckets of the three stabled horses and had a last look at Bracken. He seemed to have settled down and was munching his hay.

"We'll see how he goes, tomorrow," said Anne. "Mrs. Brown comes in the afternoon. I think Bracken will just suit her. Will you be coming after school, Katy?"

"Of course!" Katy replied. "I wish I could leave school and work for you all the time."

"I'm afraid I couldn't afford to pay you a proper wage," Anne laughed. "You'll have to wait till I've built the business up a bit. Now, off you go home, both of you, or you'll get soaked."

Katy and Clive got on their bikes and set off for home.

"Cheerio," said Clive, when he reached his gate. "See you on Saturday. I can't ride again till then, I've got loads of homework to do."

"Poor old you! 'Bye."

Katy was glad her parents understood her passion for horses and allowed her to spend all her free time at the stables.

CHAPTER TWO

A BEGINNERS' HORSE

ANNE was rather pleased with her new purchase. Bracken was certainly not a handsome horse, but, she thought, he was going to solve several problems for her. One of these problems was Mrs. Brown.

Mrs. Brown was a large lady, no longer young, who had decided to take up riding because she needed some fresh air and exercise. "And I've always *loved* horses, you know, my dear," she said to Anne.

However, finding a suitable mount for Mrs. Brown had been something of a headache. Misty, who was quiet, was not strong enough to carry the lady's weight, and Copper, who was big enough, was far from quiet. Anne had given Mrs. Brown her lessons so far on Zephyr, a horse belonging to Major Drake, which she had at livery; but this was not entirely satisfactory as she had to arrange Mrs. Brown's lessons for the times when the Major did not want to ride. Besides, she had to reduce the amount she charged the Major because she was using his horse. Anyway, Zephyr was really too good for a beginner and it was not fair on him, to have Mrs. Brown's weight flopping about on his back. Bracken, Anne thought, would be ideal.

Before Mrs. Brown came for her ride, Anne decided it would be wise to take the new horse round the paddock once or twice herself.

Bracken backed away from her when she went into the stable carrying his bridle. Anne stood quietly talking to him until he relaxed. He threw up his head and showed the whites of his eyes when she raised her hand to put the bridle over his head, so she went on talking to him and moved very slowly and quietly. Once the bridle was on he showed no more signs of fear. Anne led him out, mounted, and rode down to the paddock with no trouble at all.

The horse had obviously never had any schooling. He poked his nose and went rather stiffly, but he did not misbehave once. Anne took him back to his stable and waited for Mrs. Brown to arrive.

In a few moments a small car drove into the yard and a large lady in breeches and brown boots wriggled out of it.

"Good afternoon, Mrs. Brown," said Anne. "I think you will enjoy your ride today—I have a new horse for you to ride."

"Anne, my dear, how marvellous," gushed Mrs. Brown. "It's so exciting, riding different horses."

"Come along and meet him," said Anne, leading

the way to Bracken's stable. She opened the door and led the horse out.

"Oh, dear!" exclaimed Mrs. Brown. "He's awfully big. I do hope I won't fall off—it would be such a long way to fall."

"Of course you won't fall off," Anne replied. "Bracken is as quiet as a lamb."

Mrs. Brown suddenly thrust out her hand, intending to stroke Bracken's head. The horse threw up his head and backed away, terrified.

"Goodness!" said Mrs. Brown, in alarm. "What a nervous creature. He can't be safe to ride—you surely don't intend putting me on that animal?"

"He's perfectly safe to ride, Mrs. Brown," Anne assured her. "I'm sorry—I forgot to warn you that he doesn't like anyone to raise their hand near his head. Now, if you'd care to mount, we'll begin the lesson."

Mrs. Brown approached Bracken with suspicion, but he stood like a rock while she mounted and did not fidget once while the stirrups and girths were adjusted, so she soon began to feel more confident.

The lesson was a great success. Mrs. Brown made more progress than ever before, and was so happy about it that she booked two lessons for the following week instead of one.

When Katy arrived at the stables after school, Anne told her what a marvellous beginners' horse Bracken had turned out to be. But Katy was not very much interested in Bracken. She was still disappointed that Anne had not bought a show pony.

"I shall put Heather Clark on Bracken on Saturday," Anne said. "She's rather nervous and I think he'll give her confidence. Now, are you going to ride Biscuit again tonight?"

Katy caught and saddled Biscuit, and Anne saddled a young black horse called Zulu, which she had just broken-in. He was one of the three stabled horses, and was rather fresh. They rode down to the paddock together and had a lively hour's schooling, as Biscuit was only too ready to follow Zulu's bad example and misbehave.

"It would really have been better if you had ridden Bracken," Anne remarked. "He would have been a good influence on Zulu."

"I don't want to ride a beginners' horse!" Katy retorted.

"Katy, if you want to *work* with horses, you have to ride whatever horse you are told."

"Yes, Anne," Katy replied meekly. "Sorry. Do you want me to go and fetch him?"

"No, don't bother just now," Anne said, "but I think you should realize that working with horses isn't all fun and games."

"Oh, yes, I do know that, and I don't mind a bit. Honestly, it's the only thing I want to do," Katy protested. "*When* can I start working for you?"

"I've told you, Katy, as soon as I can afford to pay you. I want to build Danepark Stables up into a really good riding school, with an indoor school and a cross-country course. But it will take time. I'd take you on as a working pupil, if your parents would consider that."

"That would be super," said Katy. "You mean you would teach me in return for the work I did, but I wouldn't get paid?"

"That's about it," Anne replied. "I should have to pay you a little pocket money, of course. Anyway, I'll think about it, and you talk it over with your parents. Now then, come along, we'd better get back up to the stables. There's some mucking out to do."

Katy got to work on Misty's and Zephyr's stables, while Anne did Zulu's and Bracken's. When they had finished, Anne said:

"I think I will turn Bracken out with the ponies tomorrow. I can't afford to keep a horse in the stables longer than necessary, and he seems to have settled down well."

"Yes, I should think he's been used to living out," Katy remarked.

So, next morning, Anne led Bracken down to the field and turned him loose with the other ponies. She stayed to watch for a little while, to make sure there was no kicking. The others came over to investigate their new companion, but he was only interested in the juicy, green grass, and took no notice of them, so they soon wandered away to resume their grazing.

Bracken was not needed that day, so it was not until Saturday that Anne went to catch him. Katy, Clive and one or two of the other children were with her. They all carried halters and had their pockets full of oats.

"Clive, you catch Whiskey," said Anne. "Katy can catch Biscuit, that leaves Copper and Topsy for the rest of you and I'll catch Bracken."

They all divided up and went to catch their ponies. Bracken was on his own at the far end of the field, and by the time Anne reached him the others were all haltered, as they were used to coming to be caught when called.

Bracken did not seem to hear or notice Anne until she was almost up to him, then he threw up his head and looked at her in terror.

"All right, Bracken, old boy," she said soothingly, "I've only come to fetch you in—nothing to worry about."

She hid the halter behind her back and approached very quietly, but before she could reach him he had wheeled round and galloped away.

"Confound the animal!" said Anne. "I should have guessed he'd be difficult to catch, being so nervous of people. Why on earth didn't I keep him in? Or at least leave a headcollar on him."

She walked quietly after him, but it was impossible to get within yards of him. She went back to the stables to recruit some helpers.

Katy, Clive and a boy called Peter went back with her to the field.

"Now, we must be very careful how we go about this," Anne told them. "We don't want to frighten him. Spread out and drive him very slowly towards the far corner. There's a very high, thick hedge just there, and we'll have him cornered. Try not to let him go out of a walk, and if he does, whatever you do don't run after him."

The plan seemed to be working very well. They drove him quietly towards the corner, but as he got near to it and the fan of people began to close in towards him, he suddenly broke into a canter, stood back at the hedge, and, with an enormous leap, sailed clean over.

CHAPTER THREE

THE RUNAWAY

"FANTASTIC!" Clive said, for the umpteenth time. "I have never seen a horse jump so high."

"You're not the only one, Clive," said Anne. They, and as many of the other children as were sufficiently good riders, were riding across the fields on Bracken's trail.

"He must have gone like the wind," Katy remarked, "to have got out of sight so quickly. Where can he be?"

"I only wish I knew, Katy," Anne replied. "We shall reach the main road very soon. He must have crossed that. If we haven't seen him by the time we reach a telephone box, I will phone the police. He might cause an accident if he's loose on the road."

They came to the main road, and then to the telephone box, without having seen a sign of Bracken, so Anne dismounted, gave her reins to Katy, and telephoned the police.

"There's only one place he can be," Anne said as they continued on their way, "he must be in the forest. He can go for miles there and we'll never see him."

The forest lay just ahead of them. It was Forestry Commission land and stretched for miles.

"This is hopeless," Katy sighed. "How shall we catch him in here?"

"I wish I knew!" said Anne fervently. "Look, Katy, I think you'd better take these children back to the stables. They've had a good hour's hack now, and I don't want to lose them all in the forest. There are some beginners waiting for a lesson, too. Do you think you could manage? You were doing very well with Clive the other day."

"Gosh, Anne—you mean I can take a lesson? How super. I'd love to! Don't you worry about a thing. You and Clive just go on searching and I'll look after the stables." Katy began organizing the children, and soon had them heading back in an orderly single file.

Anne and Clive went on into the forest.

"It's rather like looking for a needle in a haystack, isn't it?" remarked Clive gloomily. "I keep seeing hoof-prints on the ground, but they may not be Bracken's. Lots of people ride through here."

Suddenly a piercing whinny made them both jump, and, looking to their right they could see a clearing in the trees, and there, head raised, staring at them, stood the big brown horse.

"What a good thing horses are gregarious," Anne observed. "A horse that has been on his own a little while will always go to join the first horse he sees. Just sit perfectly still, Clive, and wait for him to come up to us."

They sat as still as statues while Bracken began to walk slowly towards them. Then he broke into a trot and in another moment he was touching noses with Anne's horse. Anne made a slight movement to untie the halter she had fixed round her waist, but Bracken immediately sprang sideways. Anne knew she would have to be very careful.

"We'll ride on," she whispered to Clive. "If he'll follow us we can lure him into a shed or something."

They began to walk on slowly. Anne knew it was better to go on into the forest than to turn for home. If they turned back they were unlikely to halter him before they reached the main road, but a little further ahead she remembered there was a wood-yard where the timber was sawn up. She just hoped there would not be any men working there who might frighten him away.

Bracken fell into step behind them. Clive and Anne rode quietly on, appearing to ignore him. At last they reached the wood-yard and Anne was pleased to see it was silent and deserted. The high, wooden gates stood open. They went in and Bracken followed.

"Now," Anne whispered, "if he'll follow me past these stacks of timber, you go back, very quietly, and close the gates."

Clive halted Whiskey, while Anne rode on. At first Bracken hesitated, beside Clive, but then, seeing the tail of Anne's mount disappearing round a woodpile, he changed his mind and went on. Clive heaved a sigh of relief, turned Whiskey round and went to shut the gates.

They were heavy gates, and were held back by bolts in the ground, so Clive had to dismount. He struggled with the bolts, and Whiskey grew fidgety. The second of the gates was just swinging closed when there was a clatter of hooves coming across the yard. Clive slammed the gate shut and fastened the catch and turned to see Bracken slithering to a halt. Clive was glad the gates were so high, or Bracken would surely have gone clean over them and over Clive as well.

Anne rode up. "Good boy, Clive. Well done," she said. "Now, don't move! Don't frighten him away whatever you do. We'll try and get each side of him so he can't turn round. Just move Whiskey very quietly so that he is on the left and I'll come up on the right."

They accomplished their hemming-in movement very cautiously and at last Anne was able to slip the halter rope round Bracken's neck, and eventually to get the halter on. Once caught, Bracken was his usual, docile self once more.

"This horse is a real mystery," Anne remarked as they rode home, Bracken trotting along as quietly as a big dog beside them. "I would love to know the reason for his strange behaviour. I know one thing, though, Clive—I'm not turning him out again! What a nuisance. I really don't want the expense of another stabled horse."

"Why don't you turn Misty or Zulu out?" Clive inquired.

"It wouldn't be fair to Misty. He's an old pony and is used to being stabled. I can turn Zulu out as soon as I've finished breaking him in properly. If Bracken were not so quiet to ride and therefore so useful, I'd sell him after the performance he's given today."

"Would you *really*?" Clive asked incredulously. "When he can jump like that? The hedge he jumped must have been at least five feet high. I'm sure you could train him as a show jumper."

Anne thought for a moment. "You know, Clive," she said at last, "I think you may have a point there. We'll try him jumping. Gosh—I wonder what's happening at the stables. I do hope Katy is managing all right. I promised Heather Clark a ride on Bracken today—it's lucky she doesn't come until late this afternoon. He should have recovered from his adventure by then. He certainly looks none the worse for it."

When they got back to the stables, Katy was just getting her second ride mounted.

"Hullo, Katy," said Anne, "how are things going?"

"Oh, fine," Katy replied. "Richard Green fell off, but he's not hurt. I'm glad to see you've caught Bracken."

"Yes, he gave us quite a chase." Anne led the brown horse into his stable and tied him to the manger. "I think it may do him good to be tied up for a while and left to contemplate his sins."

Anne helped Katy to get the riders mounted and Katy was very pleased when Anne said, "You can ride Biscuit if you like, Katy, and I'll take this lesson."

So life returned to normal at Danepark Stables, and Bracken, left to himself, quietly munched his hay.

CHAPTER FOUR

CLIVE'S IDEA

"I'VE been thinking about Clive's idea," said Anne to Katy one day.

"What idea?" Katy asked.

"To make Bracken into a show jumper. He certainly can jump, and if we give him plenty of practice and careful training we might enter him for Bedloe Show, just for fun."

"Marvellous!" Katy exclaimed. "I suppose you would ride him yourself?"

"Well, no," Anne replied. "I thought it might be better if you did. You see, I should have to enter the Adult class, but you could take him in the Junior Novice class, where he'd stand a much better chance."

Katy was thrilled. She had never ridden in a Horse Show and had always had her heart set on riding a show pony, but, she thought, perhaps show jumping would be even better!

Practice began next day. Anne set up some low jumps in the paddock and Katy took Bracken over them. He always jumped as though his life depended on it, and never knocked one down or refused. Each day Anne raised the jumps a little and watched Katy take Bracken round the course.

"You must lean forward a little more," Anne told Katy, "you're getting left behind when he takes off. Just keep a gentle contact with his mouth —don't hang on the reins. Push him on a little more, but otherwise leave it to him. He seems to know the job very well already."

When the schedules for the Show arrived, Katy showed one to Clive and told him proudly that she and Bracken were competing in the jumping competition.

"Jolly good!" Clive exclaimed. "I do hope you win." He studied the schedule carefully. "I say— I wonder if Anne would let me take Whiskey in the sack race?"

"I should think so," Katy replied. "Let's go and ask her now."

Anne was sitting in her office talking to Heather Clark, and as soon as Heather heard about the Show she wanted to know if she could enter too. So Anne agreed to let Clive and Heather take Whiskey and Biscuit in the Potato and Bucket and the Sack Race.

For the next two weeks they practised for the Show every minute they could spare.

"I shall come along on Zulu," said Anne. "He's too young to compete but it will be good training for him to stand and watch. We shall not need the horse-box, as it's only five miles to Bedloe. It will be a pleasant ride as there are no main roads in that direction."

The day before the Show was one of busy preparation. They gave the horses a thorough grooming and plaited their manes to make them look really smart.

"The tack must all be cleaned," said Anne. "Make sure you undo all the buckles and take it all to pieces before you start, and I shall expect to see the bridles properly put together again afterwards."

So they washed, and saddle-soaped and oiled all the leather until it shone. Katy had done quite a lot of tack cleaning before and soon had her bridle re-assembled, but Heather got into a dreadful muddle and had to ask Anne to help her. Clive said he knew how to do it, but when Anne inspected it she found he had put the nose-band on back to front and fastened the reins to the front of the bit.

"Clive!" she laughed, "I should be very interested to see how you ride Whiskey in this peculiar contraption, but I think I'd better give you a lesson on how to put a bridle together."

When at last the saddles and bridles were all hung tidily away in the tack-room, Anne said it was time they all went home.

"Be sure you all get here at half past eight to-morrow morning," she said, "and bring your lunch with you."

So Katy, Heather and Clive went home, very excited at the prospect of their first Horse Show.

CHAPTER FIVE

A RED ROSETTE

THE little village of Bedloe was very proud of its Annual Show. It had been held regularly on the last Saturday in June for twenty years. The Park of Bedloe Manor made a beautiful show-ground.

Marquees had been erected for Refreshments, Flowers and Produce and the Handicrafts Exhibition. There was a roped-off area for the Dog Show and at the far side of the Park there was a large ring for the Horse Show.

The villagers said the sun always shone for Bedloe Show and it was certainly shining now, in a sparkling blue sky, as Anne led her little band of riders into the Park.

The Show was due to begin at ten-thirty and Anne had timed it so that they arrived with half an hour to spare. They crossed the Park to the Horse Show ring and chose a shady spot under some trees where they took off their saddles and let the ponies graze.

"I'll go and find the secretary's tent," said Anne. "Heather, will you hold Zulu for me, please? Katy,

33

don't let go of Bracken whatever you do! We don't want another chase after him."

Anne found the secretary sitting at a wooden table in an open-fronted tent. He had only just arrived and had a sheaf of papers in front of him which he was trying to sort out.

"I want to make some entries, please," said Anne.

"Certainly," said the young man, "just hang on for a second while I find the entry form."

He spread the papers out and finally unfolded a large sheet which was the one he wanted.

Anne explained that she wanted to enter one horse for the Junior Novice jumping class and two ponies for two gymkhana events each. The secretary filled in the names in the appropriate columns, then dived under the table and finally emerged with a cardboard box. From this he extracted three number cards for the riders to tie on their backs.

When she had paid him the entry fees, Anne returned to the little group of ponies and children under the trees.

Heather was looking rather tense and Katy was getting a bit edgy and snapping at Clive when he spoke to her.

"I'm glad you're back!" Clive said to Anne. "Katy's been frightened to death in case Bracken

34

ran away and Heather keeps moaning because I won't hold Biscuit for her."

"Well, Zulu was trying to bite him and Biscuit nearly trod on my lunch," Heather complained.

"Now, children, don't let's have any squabbles," Anne pleaded. "This is our big day, remember. Here are your numbers—let me tie them on for you; then we'll saddle up and have a ride round."

Horse-boxes and cars with trailers were beginning to arrive now and the loudspeakers round the ring were starting to crackle and hum. Soon, their corner of the Park seemed to be filled with children, ponies and cars.

Zulu was rather excited by the crowds, and when music suddenly blared out loudly from the loudspeakers he leaped in the air and began to prance. Biscuit was on his toes, too, but Bracken and Whiskey continued to behave perfectly as always.

The first class to enter the ring was that for leading rein ponies. Then there was a children's riding class. When the show ponies came in, Katy sighed—she still longed to be among those smartly turned-out riders on beautiful ponies.

"Watch carefully," Anne advised her, "you can learn many useful things by watching other people, and I may buy that show pony you have set your heart on, one of these days."

When the showing classes were over, the

stewards came into the ring to set up poles for the gymkhana events.

"They always keep the jumping till last here," Anne told Katy, "because there are more people to watch in the afternoon."

"Don't remind me!" said Katy nervously. "All my family are coming. Oh, dear—I'll be scared to death."

"Of course you won't," Anne replied. "Bracken knows his job, and as long as you remember all I have told you you'll be perfectly all right. There's an interval now while they prepare the ring for the gymkhana, so I think we'll take the ponies back under the trees and have lunch."

The sandwiches and cakes which they had brought with them were rather limp and warm, and Clive had a packet of crisps in his pocket which were crushed into tiny crumbs.

"I wish I had asked my mother to bring my lunch in the car," Katy wailed, trying to peel a flattened banana.

"Shall I go and get some lemonade and ice-cream from the refreshment tent?" Clive suggested.

Everyone jumped at the idea and handed him their money.

"Now, don't go filling yourselves up with fizzy pop," Anne warned them, "or you'll never be able to run in those sacks."

36

When they had finished lunch and Clive had taken all the empty bottles back, a voice over the loudspeakers began to call gymkhana competitors into the collecting ring.

Soon it was the potato and bucket race, for which Clive and Heather had entered. The race was run in three heats as there were so many entries. Clive's heat was run before Heather's.

Whiskey got away to a good start, but he was rather slow on the turns. However, Clive was able to get him close to the bucket and to lean right down, so that his potato never once bounced out. The riders of some of the faster ponies were more reckless and often had to get off when their potatoes missed the bucket altogether. So when Clive crossed the finishing line first, Katy, Anne and Heather cheered loudly.

Heather was not so lucky on Biscuit. He fidgeted on the starting line and got left behind badly. Then he refused to stand still for Heather to drop her potato in and she had to dismount three times to pick it up. She crossed the finishing line a disappointed last.

"Biscuit is naughty!" Anne said to Katy. "He's had plenty of practice at home, but I expect the excitement today is too much for him."

In the final race, Clive came second to a girl on a very handy pony which was fast on the turns. He was smiling broadly as he received his rosette, and

Katy, Anne and Heather clapped as loudly as they could.

The sack race was a dismal failure, as far as Heather and Clive were concerned. Clive fell flat on his face at his first hop and Biscuit refused to be led by the strange, lurching creature which was Heather in her sack.

Clive looked very happy as he rode back to join the others, with a blue rosette proudly displayed on Whiskey's bridle, but Heather's face wore a frown.

"Well done, Clive," said Anne. "Cheer up, Heather—everyone can't win you know."

"Huh!" snorted Heather, "I thought I was a better rider than that."

"If you were not a good rider," Anne replied quietly, "I would not have allowed you to bring a difficult pony like Biscuit to a gymkhana at all. He'll learn with experience, and so will you."

So Heather was consoled.

The last event was soon over and the stewards began to erect the jumps.

"Now, Katy," said Anne, "I saw a practice jump over there. Go and take Bracken over it two or three times to loosen him up."

So Katy rode across to the place Anne had pointed out. There were several more horses and riders taking turns at jumping it, and Katy had to wait her turn.

Bracken jumped it easily three times, and as

Katy turned to ride away, a tall, bald-headed man came up and went to slap Bracken on the neck. The horse jumped away sideways and eyed the man nervously.

"Is this your horse, miss?" the man asked.

"No," Katy replied. "Please don't touch him—he's rather nervous."

"Yes," the man agreed, "I can see that. Jumps well, though."

"Very well indeed," said Katy.

The man continued to regard Bracken thoughtfully. Then a boy on a chestnut rode up.

"Hey, Dad," he said to the bald-headed man. "Watch Tartan jump once more; then I'm off to the collecting ring."

The man gave Bracken another long stare, then turned away. Katy hurried back to her friends.

On her way back to join the others, Katy met her mother, father and young brother.

"Hello, Katy," they chorused.

"My goodness, what a big horse!" her mother exclaimed. "I don't know how you dare ride him."

"Not so big, really, Mummy," Katy laughed. "It's just that you are used to seeing me on small ponies. I can't stop to talk—I have to get to the collecting ring."

"Which class are you in?" her father asked.

"It's class fourteen—rider under seventeen,

horse any height, Junior Novice Jumping. Now I must hurry. Cheerio."

Her family called "Good luck" after her as she rode away.

Katy found she was too excited to be nervous and was actually looking forward to sailing over the jumps, which she could now see as she entered the collecting ring. The other riders all looked unconcerned and none of them took any notice of her, except the boy on Tartan, who muttered "Hello", but did not smile.

She took Bracken to a quiet corner of the collecting ring to await her turn. "Good boy, Bracken," she said. "I know you will do your best, but if I fall off, please don't run away!"

The crowd in the collecting ring grew smaller and smaller as one by one the riders' numbers were called. Suddenly Katy realized she had been taking no notice of the proceedings at all—not listening for the announcements of clear rounds, or the number of faults.

"Anne told me to watch for other people's mistakes, so that I could avoid them," she said to Bracken. "Never mind, we'll just jump as if we were in the paddock at home and do the best we can."

"Hey, you on the brown horse," the boy on Tartan was shouting to her, "they're calling your number—get in the ring quick."

"Oh—oh, thank you," Katy had quite forgotten what her number was. She hurried Bracken forward and next moment she was in the ring. She cantered a small circle and was vaguely aware of a sea of faces all about her, but she soon forgot them as she gave her attention to the jumps.

First came a nice little brush fence, then a dragon's teeth, followed by a Road Closed then a white gate. At the double, Bracken put in a clever stride of his own accord which got them nicely over, and at the wall he stood back and simply flew it. Katy was really enjoying herself and was quite surprised when she found they had finished the course.

"Another clear round," boomed the loudspeaker and the crowd applauded.

"Wait in the collecting ring please, miss," said a steward as she rode out, "you'll be wanted for the jump-off."

There were four clear rounds altogether and Katy noticed that Tartan was amongst them. The bald-headed man was standing by the collecting ring, giving his son much advice.

Now Katy really felt nervous. To be in the jump-off was more than she had dared to hope for. A girl on a grey was first to jump. Katy listened to the "Ooohs" and "Aahs" of the crowd then heard the commentator announce, "Eight faults for Silver." Then a boy on a cobby piebald was called in, and in a few moments the voice crackled, "Domino is disqualified for three refusals." Katy and Bracken were next, leaving the boy on Tartan alone in the collecting ring.

Bracken achieved another faultless round. The raised height of the jumps seemed to spur him on to jump even better. Katy returned once more to the collecting ring, passing Tartan on his way out.

Katy's heart was in her mouth as Tartan jumped his round. She could see him clearing jump after jump—then, suddenly there was an "Aah" from the crowd and at last the loudspeaker announced "One refusal—three faults for Tartan."

Katy could hardly believe it! Her first show and she had won.

"It's you who are the clever one, Bracken," she whispered, patting his neck. "I would not be here at all if it were not for you."

The loudspeaker began to crackle again and called the winners into the ring to collect their prizes. Katy smiled at the boy on Tartan as he lined his horse up next to Bracken, but he gave her a cold stare. However, the girl on the grey horse smiled at Katy and said, "Well done."

The judges were grouped round a table on which stood silver cups and rosettes. A lady in a flowery hat came forward to present the prizes. Suddenly the voice over the loudspeaker said: "Hold it! Hold it! I'm sorry, ladies and gentlemen, but there

has been an objection to the winner. Will the
owner of Bracken please come to the secretary's
tent immediately?"

Katy was astonished. What on earth was going
on? Why should there be an objection? She supposed she must have done something stupid—
missed out a jump, perhaps, or jumped them in
the wrong order. So now she wasn't first after all.
She was very much afraid she might burst into
tears at any moment.

She was suddenly aware of a hand on her knee,
and, looking down, found Heather standing beside
her.

"Anne told me to come and tell you not to
worry," said Heather. "She has gone to sort things
out."

"What is it all about?" Katy gulped.

"No idea—there was nothing wrong with the
way you jumped," Heather assured her. "Don't
get upset. You did jolly well."

Anne walked into the ring just then, with the
secretary and the bald-headed man whose son was
riding Tartan. They went across to the group of
judges and stewards and Katy waited tensely while
they talked and argued. The bald-headed man was
going very red in the face and shouting and Anne
was obviously having difficulty in keeping calm.

Katy said, "I wonder what it is all about?"

The boy on Tartan heard her and said icily,

"You should know! This is supposed to be a Novice class."

"But I've only just learned to jump!" Katy protested.

The boy gave a sneering laugh. "*You* may have," he said, "but it is the horse that has to be a novice."

Before Katy or Heather could reply, the group of judges broke up. The announcer said: "The objection has been overruled. Bracken remains the winner. The Honourable Mrs. St. John Carstairs will now present the prizes."

So Katy was duly presented with her red rosette and silver cup. She led the way round the ring at a canter, but her hour of triumph had been tarnished and she could feel the quizzical stares of the spectators and thought, by their half-hearted clapping, they must think her a cheat. She wanted to find Anne as quickly as possible to solve the mystery.

CHAPTER SIX

TACK THIEVES

ANNE, Heather and Clive were all waiting for Katy by the ring-side.

"What did I do wrong, Anne?" Katy asked. She was worried and upset.

"Nothing at all, Katy. It wasn't your fault. I can't explain here. Let's go home now and I'll tell you on the way."

So they made their way across the Park, out of the big gates, and were soon on the road that led towards home.

"Now then," Anne began, "first of all, it was Mr. Stringer, the man who owns Tartan, who objected. He says Bracken won several jumping events in shows some years ago and so is not a novice. He says the horse used to belong to a man called Snowy Peters."

"Snowy Peters?" asked Clive. "Who on earth is he?"

Anne said, "According to Mr. Stringer, Snowy Peters is a local dealer. He's very tough with his horses—in fact, he sounded altogether *too* tough, I thought."

"But how did Mr. Stringer recognize Bracken?" Katy asked.

"He used to be Snowy Peters' groom," Anne told them. "Even so, he couldn't prove Bracken was the same horse, not enough to satisfy the judges, anyway. And they accepted that I didn't know anything about the horse, having bought him in a sale, so they did not disqualify us."

"What are you going to do with Bracken now?" Clive asked.

"Well, we certainly can't enter him for any more novice classes if he is the horse Mr. Stringer says he is. The first thing to do is to prove whether he is or not."

"How can we do that?" Katy queried.

"There's only one way we can—we must track down Snowy Peters and ask him. He shouldn't be too hard to find."

"Golly, that sounds exciting. Can we help?" asked Clive.

"Well, I don't really know quite how to go about it yet, but I could certainly do with some help," Anne replied. "Any bright suggestions will be gratefully received!"

So all the way home they tried to think of a way of contacting Snowy Peters.

"Put an advertisement in the Personal column of *The Times*," said Heather.

"*Horse and Hound* would be more likely," Katy suggested.

"I don't think we could really do that," Anne said. "I'd have to put such a lot of explanation in that it would be more like a letter than an advertisement."

"Probably Mr. Stringer would know where he is," Clive said.

"Yes, quite possibly he might, but I've no wish to speak to *that* gentleman again," Anne replied.

"I would," said Clive. "He doesn't know me—I'd ask him for you."

"Well——" Anne hesitated. "I suppose that would be the simplest way. If we can find his telephone number when we get back to the stables you can give him a ring."

"But what will you say, Clive?" Katy asked. "You'll have to explain why you want to find Snowy Peters."

"Yes, you can hardly ask a stranger for someone else's address without explaining why you want it," Anne said.

"I'll think of something," Clive replied, and they all lapsed into silence and deep thought for the rest of the ride home.

Whether Clive had thought of something to say to Mr. Stringer, Anne, Katy and Heather never knew, for, on arrival at the stables all thought of tracing Snowy Peters was quickly driven from their minds.

It was obvious something was wrong as soon as they entered the yard. The tack-room door was hanging drunkenly on broken hinges and two red tail-bandages lay, unrolled, in the middle of the yard.

Anne sprang from Zulu's back and handed her reins to Clive. First she looked into all the stables and was relieved to find Misty and Zephyr safe. Then she went into the tack-room.

At first she was quite stunned. It couldn't be true! All the saddle and bridle racks were empty, and the bags of grooming kit gone. There was not so much as a spare stirrup leather left in the place.

Katy, Clive and Heather sat silently waiting for Anne to come out and tell them what had happened. When she did reappear her face was quite expressionless but white as a sheet.

"We've been robbed," she said simply.

"Robbed?" echoed Katy. "What have they stolen?"

"Every bit of tack which was here. Put the horses away. I'm going to phone the police."

Katy, Heather and Clive dismounted in stunned silence and unsaddled the ponies. When Clive and Katy returned from turning Whiskey and Biscuit out in the paddock, Anne and Heather were busy mixing feeds for the stabled horses.

"The police will be here in a few moments," Anne told them. "Apparently there has been a lot of tack stealing going on all over the country."

"What will you do?" Katy asked. "You'll not have enough saddles and bridles when all the children come to ride tomorrow."

"I know," Anne replied. "Four saddles and four bridles between eight horses. They will just have to take turns with what we have got."

"What about the Major's tack?" Katy asked. "That beautiful double bridle and spring tree saddle must be worth a lot of money."

"I've thought of that," said Anne. "I only hope he had them insured and doesn't hold me responsible."

A neat black car drove into the yard and two policemen climbed out. Anne turned to Katy: "Take these feeds to the horses for me, and Clive and Heather can fill the water buckets, while I talk to the police."

Anne showed the policemen into her office and the children went off to see to the horses.

"What an awful thing to have happened!" Heather said, when they had finished and were sitting in the hay barn waiting for Anne. "What a good job you two came to the show, or Whiskey's and Biscuit's tack would have been stolen too."

"I'd like to get hold of those thieves!" said Katy angrily. "Just when Anne was getting the riding school going and beginning to make it pay, and now she will have to buy more saddles and bridles and grooming kit."

Anne came out of the office and the policemen got into their car and drove away.

"What happened? What did they say? Do you think they'll catch the thieves?" The children all questioned Anne at once.

"They haven't much hope of catching them," Anne replied. "They think it is a highly organized gang, but they cannot find where their head-quarters are, or how they get rid of the stuff. In some parts of the country even ponies have been stolen."

"How awful!" Katy cried. "If they stole any of yours I'd just die!"

"Let's hope they don't come near us again," said Anne. "Now, my first problem will be to replace the tack. Of course I had it insured, so I will contact the insurance people tomorrow. Then we'll see if there's a sale on anywhere where I can pick up some second-hand saddles."

"Ooh, can I come?" Katy pleaded. "I've never been to buy saddles."

"I'll think about it," Anne promised. "Now, off home all of you. You've had quite enough excitement for one day."

CHAPTER SEVEN

A MEETING WITH SNOWY PETERS

MONDAY was rest day at Danepark Stables and Anne was sitting in her office reading *Horse and Hound* when Katy arrived after school.

"I like Mondays," said Katy, flinging herself into a chair. "We have the stables all to ourselves then."

"But you don't get a ride on Mondays," Anne protested. "You are very good to come and help me with the mucking-out and feeding."

"I love it," Katy replied. "It's so quiet with no one else here."

"I finished the tack cleaning in half the time today," Anne remarked, "which was not surprising, as I only had half the tack left to clean! By the way, Katy, I suppose you couldn't get Thursday off school, could you?"

"If it's for horses—yes, you bet I can!" Katy replied. "What is it?"

"Well, there's a horse sale at Flixham. I just saw a notice about it in *Horse and Hound*. It's a long way to go, but we might get some good second-hand saddles there. I don't want you to play truant from school, though. Can you get permission to stay away?"

"Let me see—Thursday—" said Katy thoughtfully. "Yes! Yes, I'm sure I can. It's Sports Day and I'm not in any of the races. The Games Mistress knows riding is the only sport I'm interested in, and she likes horses herself. I'm sure she'll let me off as I'd only be watching and not taking part. How marvellous! I've always wanted to go to a horse sale."

"Well, just make sure you get permission from school first," said Anne. "We shall have to leave here early—about eight o'clock—and we'll take our lunch with us. I will cancel the evening rides in case we are late back."

Katy was much excited and could hardly wait for Thursday. When it came at last, it was cold and wet. Katy arrived at the stables at a quarter to eight.

"It looks as though Sports Day will be cancelled," she told Anne, "but it's too late now; I've got permission to have the day off!"

Anne had fed and watered the horses and the Land-Rover stood ready in the yard.

"Off we go, then," she said. "Climb in, Katy, and settle back for a long drive."

They left Danepark Stables behind them and drove through steady, pounding rain. The wet road stretched endlessly before them and the windscreen wipers rhythmically swished to and fro. After an hour Katy had fallen asleep.

Anne woke her by slamming the door after parking the Land-Rover in a big yard next to the cattle market at Flixham.

"Here we are, Katy," she laughed, "you certainly didn't see much of the scenery on the way here!"

"Oh!" Katy yawned. "I'm so sorry, Anne. I didn't mean to fall asleep. I suppose it's because I was so excited I hardly slept all night."

"Well, come on now. Hop out! Let's go and have a look round."

The rain had stopped but the yard was full of puddles. Some very wet and bedraggled ponies were huddled together in a pen.

"Those are unbroken youngsters," Anne told Katy. "The riding ponies are in stalls in that large building across the yard."

"Oh, do let's go and see them," Katy begged.

It was a long building with stalls on each side of a passageway. In the stalls were horses and ponies of every shape and size.

"Let's see which one we would buy, if we had come to buy a pony today," said Anne. "It will test your 'eye for a horse'."

They walked up and down, discussing the good and bad points of each animal. They watched prospective buyers trying them out round the paddock outside. Katy decided on a bright bay with very showy action, but Anne said it looked rather excitable and she chose a well-mannered dapple grey.

"Enough of looking at horses we can't afford," Anne exclaimed. "We must go and look for some tack which we can!"

The saddlery was set out for inspection in an upstairs room above the Sale Ring. It was crowded with would-be buyers.

"There's a nice saddle," said Katy, pointing to one, "it would fit Topsy."

Anne lifted the flaps and pulled at the girth straps.

"The leather seems sound," she remarked. She turned it upside down and saw that the lining was good. Then she took the pommel in one hand and the cantle in the other and pressed hard. "No good," she declared, replacing it hurriedly on its rack. "The tree is broken."

"But it looks such a smart little saddle!" Katy protested.

"Better to buy a shabby one with a sound tree," Anne told her. "You can patch the leather, and re-line, or re-stuff a saddle, but if the tree is broken, the saddle is useless."

In the end, Anne picked out three saddles which she considered worth bidding for, and made a note of their Lot numbers so that she would not forget.

Then they went across the room to look at bridles.

"This snaffle bridle would do for Topsy," said Anne, "and there's a good pelham which would fit Copper. In fact there are several useful bridles here. I must jot down the Lot numbers so I know which items to bid for when the auction starts."

"It must be exciting!" Katy said. "I do hope no one else bids for the things you want."

"Oh, you may be sure they will," Anne laughed. "There are a lot of hard-bitten old dealers here today, but they won't pay over the value for anything. They usually want cheap saddles to sell with their ponies at a good profit."

Anne and Katy wandered over to the balcony which overlooked the horse sale ring below. The auction had commenced down there and the auctioneer was calling for bids as a man trotted one horse after another up and down. Bidding seemed to be slow, but Anne noticed a man in a green coat and checked cap who put in a bid for every horse that came up, but always dropped out if the bidding went very high.

A slim girl in a red shirt and blue skirt came up and leaned on the rail next to Katy. She looked lonely so Anne smiled at her and asked, "Are you here to buy a horse?"

"No such luck!" said the girl ruefully. "I've got a horse at home that I can't ride and I'll never be able to afford another."

"Oh? Why can't you ride him?" Katy asked.

"It's a long story," the girl replied. "I had been saving up for years and when I had enough money I went to a nearby dealer and asked him for a horse. He only had one at a price I could afford, but he was a beauty—black, with a white star, and such a pet. I didn't know much about buying horses, of course, but I bought him. Three days later he was lame, and still is. The vet says he can't be cured, but I couldn't bear to have him put down."

"What an awful shame!" Katy said.

"You should have gone back to the dealer," said Anne, "and demanded your money back."

"I did," the girl replied, "but no one ever got a penny out of Snowy Peters."

"Snowy Peters?" Anne echoed.

"Yes, he's a local dealer. There he is, down there, buying more worn-out horses to sell to fools like me."

Anne looked down to where she pointed. The man in the green coat was Snowy Peters!

"What an amazing piece of luck!" Anne had almost forgotten about the search for Snowy Peters in the excitement and worry of having her tack stolen. "I've been wanting to trace Mr. Peters."

"Well, that sets you apart from the rest of us," the girl said, smiling.

"You had awful luck." Katy said.

"Why do you want him?" the girl asked.

"I have a horse which I believe may have belonged to him once. Can you tell me his address in case I lose him in the crowd here?"

The girl wrote the address on a scrap of paper for Anne. "It's not far from here," she said. "Only a few miles north of Flixham."

Katy tapped Anne on the shoulder. "They are going to start selling the saddlery," she said. "Let's get near the front so we don't miss anything."

"No," said Anne, "we'll stay at the back where we can see who else is bidding."

The bidding for the saddles was brisk, but Anne managed to buy the three she wanted, though she had to pay rather more for one of them than she had intended. She bought four good bridles, a headcollar and a box full of useful odds and ends—brushes, girths and saddle soap. After buying half a dozen pairs of stirrup leathers and irons, Anne said she had spent more than she had meant to and must not be tempted by anything else.

When the auction was over and Anne had paid for all her goods, she said: "We'll go and put all these things in the Land-Rover and then see if we can find Snowy Peters."

So, staggering under their load of newly acquired tack, they made their way down the stairs and out into the yard where the Land-Rover was parked. They stowed the things carefully inside, then went back to the horse sale ring. It was deserted except for a weather-beaten little man who was sweeping up. Anne approached him tentatively.

"Er—excuse me——" she began, "I wonder if you could tell me whether Mr. Snowy Peters is still here."

"Eh?" asked the little man, putting a hand to his ear and propping his broom against the wall. "What's that yer say?"

"Snowy Peters," Anne repeated, raising her voice. "Is he still here?"

"Oh, 'im!" snorted the little old man disdainfully. "No, 'e's gorn. I 'elped 'im load up them poor nags into 'is 'orse-box. Never give me a thank you for it, neither. Ah, well, 'e's a rum 'un and no mistake."

"How many horses did he buy?" Katy asked.

"Four," said the old man. "Poor critturs."

"Is he cruel to his horses, then?" Anne asked.

"I could tell you a tale or two about 'im!" said the old man with a wink. "I never seen 'osses cringe from a man like 'is do, not without they've 'ad a few beatings. If you're looking fer 'im, you watch your step, missy. Don't go tellin' 'im 'ow to treat his 'osses, nor threatening 'im with the police —'e's a nasty bit of work, take my word for it."

"Right, thank you for your advice," said Anne.

"Come along, Katy, let's go and see if we can find him."

In the Land-Rover, Anne took the piece of paper with the address on it from her pocket.

"Well, Katy," she said, "do you feel brave enough to come with me to see this unpleasant character?"

"Just try going without me!" Katy replied. "I can't wait to meet him."

Anne started up the engine. "Remember what that old man said," she told Katy, "and don't say anything to upset Snowy."

"I'll do my best," Katy promised.

So they drove out of the yard and set off for Snowy Peters' home.

Anne was pleasantly surprised when they arrived at the dealer's yard. She had expected a tumble-down cottage and a ramshackle row of stables, but it was a pleasant farm-house with a yard surrounded on three sides by loose-boxes and sheds. A rather dilapidated horse-box stood in the middle of the yard and Anne parked her vehicle next to it.

There was much whinnying and stamping of hooves coming from one of the sheds, so Anne and Katy walked over to investigate. It was dark inside, but when their eyes became accustomed to the gloom, they could see that the shed was divided into six stalls and in each one stood a horse tied up short to its manger. A bony-looking chestnut was making all the noise. He was throwing his head up as far as the short rope would allow and neighing shrilly. Then he would paw the ground, or try to kick at the horse in the next stall.

"He doesn't look very happy," Anne remarked.

Just then they heard footsteps crossing the yard, so Anne led the way out of the stable. Coming towards them was Snowy Peters. He was a thick-set man, with fair hair and a ruddy complexion.

He greeted them pleasantly: "Hello, young ladies. What can I do for you? Come to buy a horse, have you?"

"No, not exactly," Anne replied.

At that moment there came an extra loud whinny and a clatter from inside the stable.

"Excuse me for a moment," said Snowy. "It's a horse I've just bought—he's not settled down yet."

He went into the stable and Anne and Katy followed. The chestnut kicked out as Snowy approached it, so he picked up a stiff yard broom and beat the horse across the hind legs with it. Each time the horse lashed out he repeated the dose, until the chestnut, lathered and trembling, stood still. Then he walked up to its head and whacked it four or five times across the ears.

Anne and Katy looked at each other. Remembering the advice of the old man at the sales, Anne put a finger to her lips, but Katy could not control herself.

"Leave him alone!" she cried. "You mustn't hit him like that."

Snowy came out from the chestnut's stall. "Just you mind your own business, young lady!" he said, his face redder than ever with anger. "A vicious horse needs teaching who's master, and I've mastered more vicious horses than you've ever seen!"

"Yes, yes, I'm sure you have," said Anne hurriedly. "Katy didn't mean to interfere—it's just that she's very fond of horses."

"All right then," said Snowy. "But now, do you want to buy a horse or not?"

"Well, no, I'm afraid we don't," Anne replied. "But I have a horse which I think you may have owned and I wanted you to identify him for me."

"My dear young lady!" said Snowy impatiently, "I have owned a great many horses in my time and I couldn't possibly remember what they all look like."

"I think you would know this one," Anne told him, "I believe you taught him to jump."

"Oh, did I?" Snowy began to show interest. "Well, I had a number of jumpers, you know. What does he look like and why do you think he belonged to me?"

"He's a big, brown gelding, with a slight Roman nose and rather thick in the hind legs. He's very quiet to ride but difficult to catch, and nervous of people. A man named Stringer, who said he was your groom, recognized him."

Snowy was thoughtful for a moment. "Did Stringer send you here?" he asked.

"Yes," said Anne—then realized this was not true, but Stringer's name seemed to have some influence with Snowy Peters.

"Well, it sounds a bit like a horse I had called Caramel. He showed real talent for jumping but he was a nuisance. He ran away from me any time he got the chance. Wouldn't misbehave when I was in the saddle, oh, no! Jumped like a bird. But I couldn't go near him on foot unless he was tied up short. Frightened to death of the whip, too. Yes, it might be Caramel."

"I wonder how we could prove it?" Anne asked. "You see, it's rather important as I entered him for a novice class, but if he is your Caramel he wasn't eligible."

"I'll come over and have a look at him, if you live near here," Snowy offered.

"That's very kind of you, but I'm afraid I don't," Anne answered; "I live over fifty miles away."

"Well, this interests me," said Snowy. "I should like to know if it is Caramel you've got. Wait—I've got some photographs of him indoors. I'll go and fetch them."

He strode back towards the house.

"There," said Anne when he was out of sight, "he's not so frightening after all, is he?"

"No, he's being quite helpful," Katy remarked. "But I can see why Bracken is so head-shy after seeing him hit that chestnut."

"Yes, I'm sure he must have hit Bracken about the head when he was training him to jump."

"Let's look in some of these other stables while we are waiting for him," Katy suggested.

They looked into the nearest loose-box. Inside stood a young pony, its head strapped down tightly with side reins, jingling a mouthing bit in its mouth.

"Poor thing!" said Katy. "It can't move its head or neck at all. I've a good mind to go and loosen those side-reins."

"For goodness' sake don't," Anne protested. "We don't want to upset Mr. Peters again."

She opened the next door, expecting to find another row of stalls, but inside it was very dark. She could smell leather, and when she found a light switch and turned it on, she saw that it was a tack-room. But *what* a tack-room! She had never seen so much saddlery in her life. Some of it hung neatly on pegs and racks, but most of it was in a jumbled heap on the floor.

"Goodness!" Anne exclaimed. "What a tremendous number of saddles. He probably sells them."

Just then Snowy Peters appeared, hurrying back across the yard. When he saw them in his tack-room, he ran towards them, brandishing his whip.

"So, that's what you came for, is it? Spying on me, are you. Shut that door and get off my premises."

He looked so angry that Anne and Katy had no choice. They climbed quickly into the Land-Rover and drove away.

CHAPTER EIGHT

KATY'S PLAN

ANNE did not speak to Katy until they were out of sight of Snowy Peters' farm-house. Then she slowed the Land-Rover to a more reasonable speed and said:

"Well, really, he had me quite scared."

Katy began to giggle. "His face was so red!" she spluttered. "And he was waving his whip about like a madman. Do you think he would have hit us with it?"

"I'm almost sure he would!" Anne replied. "I know it was rather nosy of us and he probably thought we were snooping, but he didn't give us much chance to explain. We must have looked like a couple of frightened rabbits!"

They both began to laugh as they pictured themselves running from the red-faced, angry man.

At last Anne said, "Of course, the trouble is that now we'll never know about Bracken. We can't possibly go back there. What a nuisance—if only we had not been so inquisitive! He was being so helpful, too. I only wanted to see if he had any nice ponies."

E

"I suppose he thought we were looking to see if he was cruel to them, but we were only looking at his tack. Why should he be so cross about that?" asked Katy.

"I wonder," said Anne. "Surely he didn't think we were going to steal any of it—we don't look like tack thieves, do we?"

"Tack thieves!" Katy exclaimed. "That's it. Maybe he's connected with the tack thieves. There was such a lot of saddlery there, far more than he could possibly want. Maybe it's stolen!"

"Well——" said Anne thoughtfully, "that is possible, I suppose. Perhaps the thieves bring it to him to dispose of. He could easily sell it, being a dealer. Goodness, Katy, what can we do about it? He may have all my stuff there; then I could recognize it and prove it was stolen. Oh, if only we hadn't upset him like that!"

"I dare go back!" said Katy, with a show of bravado. "We could take a policeman with us."

"We haven't enough proof to go to the police," Anne replied. "You can't accuse someone of stealing just because he has a lot of saddles!"

"I wonder if Clive and Heather would go and have a look. Snowy Peters doesn't know them," Katy suggested.

"Hmm. I don't know about that," Anne replied. "I would not want them to get into any sort of trouble on my account. No, I couldn't ask them to do that."

Katy said, "Very well," but she had made up her mind to ask her two friends to help.

They drove on in silence, towards Danepark Stables, which was still so many miles away. When at last they drove into the stable yard it was almost dark. The horses whinnied when they heard Anne's voice.

"All right, my beauties," she called to them. "I know you are waiting to be fed. Just wait while we put this tack away."

She and Katy carried the new saddles and bridles to the tack-room and hung them up. Then they mixed feeds and took them to the horses, filled water buckets and shut the stable doors for the night.

"I'll see you tomorrow after school," said Katy. "Many thanks for taking me. It was the most exciting day of my life. I've always wanted to be a detective!"

"Now then, Katy," Anne said, "we're not playing at detectives. But we must find some way of getting back into Snowy Peters' tack-room to see if he has my saddles. The Major's saddle would be easy to identify—it has the maker's name and a number on a metal tag under the flap."

"Oh?" said Katy. "Do you know what the number is?"

"Yes, it's an easy one to remember," Anne replied, "I used to notice it every time I cleaned the saddle—it's 876543."

"Good," said Katy, "I won't forget that. Don't worry, Anne. I'll think of a way to get your saddles back."

Anne laughed. "I wish you could, Katy. Good-bye, glad you enjoyed the trip."

Katy had already decided what to do, and as soon as she left the stables she went straight to Clive's house.

Clive was very much surprised to see her. "What on earth are you doing here at this time of night?" he asked.

Katy explained hurriedly about the visit to Snowy Peters' yard and the need for a return trip to have a better look at the saddles and bridles there.

"But, you see," she concluded, "Anne and I can't go back or he'd be suspicious at once. I wondered if you and Heather could go."

Clive stared at her in amazement. "All the way to Flixham?" he said. "How would we get there?"

"By train," Katy replied. "You'd have a lovely long train ride." She knew he had a weakness for train-spotting.

"Well—yes, I suppose we could," said Clive doubtfully. "But what can we say to Snowy Peters when we get there?"

"Say you want to buy a pony," answered Katy. "Then tell him you need a saddle for it, and get him to let you into his tack-room. I'm sure you'll think of something."

"Do you think Heather will come with me?" asked Clive.

"Of course she will! It will be jolly exciting. Now, find a piece of paper and a pencil and I will write down full instructions for you of how to find the place, and the number on Major Drake's saddle so you won't forget it. By the way, don't tell Anne you're going, and don't let her know I asked you. Cheerio."

Clive watched Katy disappearing down the garden path and realized there was nothing else for it—he'd just have to go to Flixham.

"I may as well go and see Heather right away," he thought. "If she's prepared to do it, I'm game."

Heather was all in favour of the idea. "It's a marvellous idea of Katy's, to ask us to go," she said. "Let's go on Saturday morning. I'll find out what time the trains run. Take plenty of money, and some food to eat on the way."

Clive felt rather like a Secret Agent. He hoped Katy's plan would work, and that he and Heather would not fall into enemy hands!

CHAPTER NINE

A NEW PUPIL

ON Saturday morning Katy was busy helping Anne with the grooming and saddling-up, ready for the first ride. She was kept too occupied to have time to worry much about how Clive and Heather were getting on.

"There is a new boy coming today," said Anne. "His name is David and as he is rather tall I think we will put him on Bracken."

"Is he a beginner?" Katy asked.

"Well, he says he has done a lot of riding, but I never take chances with people until I have actually seen them ride," Anne replied. "I'll give a half-hour lesson in the paddock and then take them all for half an hour's hack."

The riders soon arrived and Anne and Katy saw them all safely mounted, adjusted stirrups, tightened girths. Everyone was ready but Bracken's rider had not arrived.

"This is a nuisance," said Anne, looking at her watch. "David is late. I do like to get rides started on time or it makes us late all day and some people have buses to catch. I will wait five minutes for him but no longer."

At the end of five minutes there was still no sign of David, so Anne said she would take the ponies down to the paddock and begin the lesson. She asked Katy to wait in the yard and help David mount when he arrived.

"Bring him to the paddock to join us when he's ready," Anne said. She mounted Zulu and led her pupils in single file.

Katy began sweeping the yard. A few minutes later she heard footsteps, and, looking up to see who it was, she saw a tall fair-haired young man.

"Oh, good morning," said Katy politely. "Are you David?"

"Yes," he replied. "David Dixon. Are you one of the grooms?"

"Well, sort of," Katy smiled. "Anne has started the lesson without you, as you are late. I'll get your horse for you and take you down to the paddock."

Katy led Bracken out from his stable, and David looked rather disappointed when he saw that the heavily-built, Roman-nosed animal was to be his mount.

"I say!" he exclaimed. "Is this the only one left?"

"Yes," said Katy, "but you were going to ride him anyway, even if you'd come early. He's a jolly nice horse—he can't help it if he's not handsome."

"Humph!" David snorted. "I'm used to thoroughbreds, not common animals like that."

"Don't be so rude about Bracken!" Katy cried. "Let me tell you he shows a lot of talent as a jumper."

"Really?" David laughed derisively. "What sort of talent—knocking all the jumps down?"

Katy was getting really angry. "Well, are you going to ride him or not?" she demanded. "Because if you stand here insulting Bracken much longer I shall lose my temper!"

"If this is all there is, I suppose it will have to do," David replied. "I may as well ride now I'm here."

He reached out to snatch the reins from Katy. Bracken, already nervous from the sound of angry voices, threw up his head and swung round on his heels.

"You fool! You've frightened him," Katy shouted. "You shouldn't have grabbed at him like that."

With a clatter of hooves, Bracken bolted out of the yard and down the lane.

Anne's lesson was going rather well. The horses were all behaving themselves and the children seemed to be paying attention better than usual. She was too wrapped up in her teaching to think about the new pupil who should have joined the ride on Bracken.

She was, therefore, surprised when she saw a

very agitated Katy come running towards the paddock gate, waving her arms and shouting. Anne halted her ride and went across to the gate to inquire what was wrong.

Katy was breathless from running. "It's Bracken!" she panted, "David frightened him and he's run away."

"Oh, no!" Anne cried in despair. "Which way has he gone?"

"Up the lane, towards Elm Farm," Katy replied.

"Get on the phone to the farm," said Anne, "and ask them to look out for him. I'll take the ride up that way to look for him. We were just going for a hack, anyhow. You stay in the lane and if he comes back drive him into the yard."

Anne hurriedly gathered her pupils together and led them out towards the lane, while Katy ran back to the stables.

Katy telephoned the farm, then took up her post in the lane outside the stables. She didn't know where David had gone, but supposed he had gone home, as there was no sign of him.

"Wretched boy!" she said to herself. "It's all his fault—and then he just calmly goes home."

She stood in the lane for a long time. It was very boring and she grew tired of standing, so she sat on the grass verge.

Meanwhile, Anne and her riders were trotting up the lane towards the farm. There was no sign of Bracken, and beyond the farm the lane petered out into a mere cart track. Anne thought to herself how lucky it was that Bracken had taken this route, and not the one he took on his previous escapade. At least there was no main road ahead, and no forest.

The farmer came out at the sound of hooves. "Looking for that horse, are you, miss? I've had the young lady on the phone about it, but we haven't seen him up here. He must have turned off into one of the fields between your place and mine. Anyway, we'll watch out for him."

"Thank you very much," said Anne, and turned her party back towards home.

Katy was sitting in the grass watching a blackbird. She had kept so still that he hopped right up, quite close to her, his beady eyes glinting. Suddenly Katy heard hoofbeats. She jumped up and the blackbird flew off with a loud chattering cry.

Katy placed herself in the middle of the lane and hoped she would be able to turn Bracken, if it were he, into the yard, and that he wouldn't charge past her. The cantering hooves steadied to a trot and then a sedate walk and she began to wonder whether it could be a loose horse after all. Then, round a bend in the lane, Bracken appeared—but what a surprise for Katy! There, astride the brown horse, sitting happy and relaxed, was David.

His bowler hat, at a rakish angle on his head, was dented and some leafy twigs were sticking out at one side. There were scratches on David's face and his boots were muddy, but he smiled at Katy.

"It's great to be back in the saddle," he remarked. "Do you know, it must be two years since I last rode a horse?"

"Oh," said Katy, too stunned for the moment to think of anything else to say.

"He's cut his leg a bit," said David. "I don't think it's bad. I'll put him in his stable, shall I?"

Just then, Anne and her riders came into the yard.

"You've caught him!" Anne said thankfully. "How did you manage it?"

"Well," David began, "I just followed him up the lane. I thought your groom would be coming, but she didn't appear."

"No," Katy explained, "I went to tell Anne."

"Oh, well, anyway, he disappeared in the distance, but I kept going until at last I saw him grazing in a field. I went up to him, but he dashed off again and jumped a hedge into the next field with me in hot pursuit. At the end of the field were a great big thorny hedge and a ditch and I expected those to stop him, but nothing of the sort—he flew over them! Only, luckily for me, his reins caught in the hedge and brought him down. I scrambled over after him and he soon calmed down so that I could free the reins. I got him up and he seemed quite okay except for that small cut."

"I'm most grateful to you," said Anne. "This is the second time he has run away. He gave us an awful chase last time."

Katy opened Bracken's stable door and David led him in.

"I'm sorry I was rude about him," David said, "he's really a very enjoyable ride, even if he's not handsome. I shall look forward to riding him again."

"Next time you come," Anne smiled, "I suggest that you come early. I always start my rides on time."

"I'll remember that," David replied. "I'm very sorry I was late today."

At last the day's rides were finished and all the riders gone home. Katy helped Anne to feed and water the horses, but for once she was anxious to go home. Anne thought it strange, but said nothing.

Katy left the stables and hurried to Clive's house, hoping he and Heather had returned safely from Flixham.

Heather and Clive were sitting in the kitchen at Clive's house drinking hot chocolate and munching biscuits.

"Thank goodness you are both back all right," said Katy, sitting down and helping herself to a gingernut.

Clive poured some milk into a saucepan and mixed her a hot drink. "I didn't realize you were worried about us," he said. "After all, it was your idea."

"Of course it was," Katy said, "but if anything had happened to you, Anne would have been furious with me."

"Well, don't worry," Clive told her. "I think she'll be pleased with all of us when she hears. Snowy Peters definitely has the Major's saddle, and I'm sure Anne's saddles and bridles are there too."

"Do tell me all about it!" Katy pleaded. "How did you get in the tack-room?"

"It wasn't easy," Clive replied.

"The trouble was," said Heather, "he didn't seem to believe at first that we had really come to buy a pony. He wanted to know why our parents weren't with us."

"I told him they didn't like horses," Clive said, "but had said we could buy one as long as it didn't bother them. He brought out some awful old hacks to start with—poor old things that should have been pensioned off. But he soon realized that we knew a bit about horses, so then he showed us two nice ponies, a bay and a grey."

"I really would have liked to buy the grey," said Heather. "He let me ride it, and it was super."

"How did you get out of buying it, then?" Katy asked.

"We didn't try to, at first," Clive replied. "I said we should need a saddle for it, if we bought it. Snowy said we could have the one that it had on, so I had to say I didn't like that one. He fetched another one and I said it wasn't a good fit. When he went to take it back I followed him into the tack-room. He wasn't very happy about it and tried to hurry me out, but he couldn't say much because he thought I was going to pay him a lot of money. At last I saw one I said I liked—I'm sure it was one of Anne's, the one Misty used to wear—and asked him to go and put it on the pony while I looked for a bridle. While he was gone I had a quick look round. I found Major Drake's saddle and bridle covered up with a horse blanket. It was his all right, I checked the number. That was all the evidence we needed, so the next thing was to get away."

"That was the worst part!" said Heather. "He had been very nice to us up till then. When Clive said that we would come back in a day or two if we decided to buy the pony, Snowy Peters went so red in the face I thought he'd burst."

"Golly, were you scared?" asked Katy. "Anne and I were frightened to death when he got angry with us."

"Well, I thought it best to leave as quickly as possible," Clive told her. "I looked at my watch and said, 'I'm sorry, we must rush off or we shall miss our train.' Heather and I left him holding the pony and tore out of his gate."

"I was petrified," Heather admitted. "We ran and ran and I kept expecting to hear him coming after us."

"We went straight to the nearest police station," Clive continued. "I told them all about it and they promised to investigate at once. They were very nice, though I'm sure they thought we were quite mad. Do you know, they even drove us to the station in a black police car, and saw us on to the train. I gave them Anne's telephone number and they promised to ring her as soon as there is any news."

"Tomorrow we must tell Anne what you did," Katy said. "She will be pleased with you, but I'm afraid she may be cross with me for asking you to go."

"Never mind," said Heather, "I don't think Anne could ever get *very* cross. I must go home now, though, because my father *can*, and he does get awfully cross if I am late."

"I must go too," Katy said. "Thanks for the hot drink, Clive. Thank you both for going to Snowy's —as a matter of fact I didn't really think you'd dare!"

Clive aimed a gingernut at her, but she ducked and it hit Heather instead.

"See you at the stables tomorrow," called Katy,

dodging out of the door before Clive could try a second shot. "Goodnight," and she hurried home.

There was no riding on Sunday mornings at Danepark Stables as Anne always went to church. In the afternoon Katy was, as usual, the first one to arrive.

Anne was looking puzzled. "I've just had a telephone call from the police," she said. "They say they think they have found my stolen saddles and bridles, and will want me to go along to identify them. I wonder if they found them at Snowy Peters', and if so, why the police went there?"

Katy looked guilty. "I can explain," she said.

She told Anne the story of Clive and Heather's trip and how she had asked them to go. Anne was silent for several minutes.

"Katy," she said sternly at last, "you know I did not want them to take such a risk. You know quite well what sort of man Snowy Peters is."

Clive and Heather arrived just at that moment. They looked so pleased with themselves that Anne had to smile. "Here come the amateur detectives, then," she laughed. "You have all been very naughty, but I am very grateful to you. If I get my tack back, I shall give you all a free ride every day for a week."

"That's okay," said Clive. "It was fun. The trouble is now I can't decide whether to be a cowboy, a train driver or a Private Eye."

CHAPTER TEN

THE TACK THIEVES CAUGHT

IT was several days before there was any news of the missing tack. Katy was helping Anne to get a group of riders mounted ready for a lesson, when a police car drew into the stable yard. Anne went across to speak to the driver, and Katy went on with the job of adjusting stirrups and girths.

Anne came back looking a little worried. "Katy," she said, "I have to go to the police station to identify some saddlery. I told them it was most inconvenient just now, but I really can't refuse as they have sent a car for me. Do you think you could manage to take this lesson? I'll be as quick as I can."

"Of course I can manage!" Katy assured her. "I did it before, didn't I? Don't worry, Anne —you go and see about getting your things back."

So Anne climbed into the car and drove off with the policemen. The riders were all agog with curiosity.

"Wherever is she going? Have they arrested her? Is she coming back?" they asked.

"Don't be silly," Katy replied. "Haven't you heard about the saddles that were stolen?"

Most of them had not, including David, who had come for another ride on Bracken. "Come on, Katy, tell us all about it," he said.

"Anne told us not to gossip about it," Katy replied, "but I suppose I had better tell you now. The tack was stolen while we were at Bedloe Show. When we went to ask Snowy Peters about Bracken——"

"Snowy Peters?" David interrupted. "What connection is there between that rogue and Bracken?"

"Why, do you know him?" Katy asked in surprise.

"Only by reputation. My uncle used to be a horse dealer up in Wales. He used to import hunters from Ireland and he sold Peters several. I remember he was most annoyed because he sold him one horse, which Uncle thought was a dud, very cheaply. Peters turned it into a jumper and probably made a lot of money with it."

"David, do you really mean that?" said Katy excitedly. "Maybe that horse was Bracken. Snowy Peters called him Caramel. Do you think your uncle would still be able to recognize him?"

"Uncle always boasts he never forgets a horse that has once been through his hands. He's retired now and frightfully old, but he comes to stay with us for a week every year," David told her. "I'll write to him as soon as I get home. He'll be keen to come when I tell him about this horse. He still can't resist being near horses."

"But why has Anne gone with those police-men?" asked one small girl. So Katy explained as briefly as possible about the hoard of saddles they had seen in Snowy Peters' tack-room.

"Now," she said, "it's time we went down to the paddock and started the lesson."

Katy did her best to give the kind of lesson she knew Anne would have given, but she found it difficult to be as patient as Anne. Some of the riders just didn't seem to listen to what she said, and she had to say "Keep your heels down" so many times to the little girl on Topsy that she began to wonder if the child knew the difference between heels and toes. She was afraid the boy on Misty might fall off at any moment, as he would keep leaning forward no matter how often she told him to sit back. When the lesson was over, she was quite relieved, but the riders all seemed to have enjoyed it and chatted and laughed amongst them-selves on the way back to the stables.

Anne had not returned, so Katy organized the children and soon had them unsaddling and rub-bing down their ponies, filling hay nets and water buckets. She was just beginning to wonder whether Anne would be back in time for the next ride, when the telephone in the office rang. Katy thought it might be Anne and ran to answer it.

"Is that Danepark Stables?" asked the voice at the other end of the line.

"Yes," Katy replied. "Can I help you?"

"This is Miss Tomkins, from Highfield Girls' School," said the voice. "I want to arrange for some riding lessons."

"Just a moment while I find the appointments book," said Katy. She found it, and a pencil, and returned to the telephone. "When would you like to come?"

"On Tuesday and Thursday afternoons," said Miss Tomkins. "There will be twelve girls each time."

"Oh—oh, yes, I see," said Katy, trying not to sound too surprised. "Very well then, two-thirty on Tuesdays and Thursdays, I will make a note of that. Thank you."

Only when she had hung up the receiver did it occur to Katy that Anne did not possess twelve ponies. "Oh, gosh!" she thought. "I am stupid. I should have asked her to ring again when Anne was here. What *will* Anne say?"

Anne, as it happened, was much pleased. "That's marvellous, Katy," she said. "Now perhaps we can really start to expand. Twenty-four extra pupils a week will make it worth while buying some more ponies. Then I will advertise in the local paper—that should bring in some more riders. Now, let me tell you my news."

"Oh, yes, do," Katy begged. "Have they put Snowy Peters in prison?"

"Not yet, but I'm sure they will. It seems he did not actually steal the tack himself, but he employed other men to steal it for him," Anne told her. "Another thing, Katy, when the police searched his premises they found plenty of evidence of his cruelty, and he is to be banned from keeping horses any more."

"I'm very glad about that!" Katy declared. "Have you got your saddles and bridles back?"

"Not yet," Anne replied. "They are needed as evidence, but I shall get them back as soon as the case is over and Snowy Peters is safely locked away in prison. There is just one thing worrying me now, though. How shall we ever prove whether Bracken is really Caramel or not, with Snowy in gaol?"

Katy smiled. "I've got that all arranged," she said, and told Anne about David's uncle.

"Katy," said Anne, "you're a marvel! What should I do without you?"

"I don't know," Katy laughed, "but don't forget I'm coming to work for you when you expand your riding school."

"You certainly are," Anne replied. "I wouldn't have anyone else!"

CHAPTER ELEVEN

BRACKEN IS CARAMEL

D AVID'S Uncle Steve was a small, white-haired old man with twinkling blue eyes. He stood in the yard at Danepark Stables and took a deep breath.

"Ah," he sighed. "There's no better smell in the world than the smell of horses."

Anne showed him round the stables. He admired Zephyr and Zulu and complimented Anne on the way she looked after her horses. Then Anne led him into Bracken's stable.

"This is the one I want you to look at," she said. "Have you ever seen him before?"

The old man stared hard at Bracken. "I remember this horse!" he exclaimed. "Came over with a bunch from Ireland. Ugly beast, and nervous, too. I sold him to some chap who made a show jumper out of him."

"Would that have been Snowy Peters?" Anne asked.

"Can't rightly remember the fellow's name now," said Uncle Steve, scratching his head. "Peters—yes, I believe that it was. He had a nasty way with his horses, he did. I never would have sold him a horse at all if I'd known he was that sort. Paid me next to nothing for this animal, and treated him fierce."

"Thank you very much for coming to look at him for me," said Anne. "Now I know he is really Caramel, I shall register him with the Show Jumping Association as Bracken. Then I can enter him in big shows. If he wins, it will be good publicity for Danepark Stables."

Uncle Steve wished her luck and said good-bye.

Anne had arranged to go and see two ponies which were for sale, and she took Katy with her.

The ponies belonged to a family called Oakley who had a small farm not many miles from the riding school. Mrs. Oakley took Anne and Katy to a big meadow where a bay and a skewbald were grazing. She called: "Dandy, Jester, here, come along." They both threw up their heads and looked at her. Then they cantered across the meadow and came to a slithering halt almost on top of Mrs. Oakley.

"They are great pets," she said. "We have had them both for five years. My two daughters used to ride them a lot but they have both left school now and have not the time to ride, so the ponies do nothing but stand about and eat!"

"It must be very sad to have to part with them," Anne remarked.

"It is indeed," Mrs. Oakley replied. "I want to be quite sure they go to a good home."

"They would have a good home with me," Anne assured her; "I have kept horses for many years and I take the greatest care of them."

Mrs. Oakley slipped halters on to the ponies and led them up to the farmyard.

"I will saddle them up and you can try them," she said. "I suppose you will only want to buy one of them. It will be such a pity to part them, as they are firm friends."

"No," said Anne, "I would buy them both if they are suitable. I want several more for my riding school."

Mrs. Oakley frowned. "Oh, dear," she said. "I didn't know you had a riding school. These ponies are used to a private home—I shouldn't like to think of them being pulled about by lots of children."

Katy was indignant. "The horses at Danepark Stables are never pulled about. They are very well cared for, and Anne never lets people ride unsupervised."

"I'm sorry," said Mrs. Oakley. "I didn't mean to offend you in any way, but I do want to be sure that Dandy and Jester go to a good home."

"Of course you do," Anne said, "I quite understand. If I buy your ponies you would be quite welcome to come and visit them at any time."

"Oh—well, thank you!" Mrs. Oakley exclaimed. "And, of course, I suppose my daughters could come and ride them at week-ends, couldn't they? Now, which will you try first?"

"I'll try the bay," Anne replied.

He was a smart pony, about fourteen hands, and Anne found him a willing, easy ride. The skewbald, who was a little bigger, she soon discovered to be rather lazy, but she decided they would both be useful animals to have in the riding school. Mrs. Oakley was asking quite a reasonable price for the pair, so Anne made a deal with her and bought both ponies, complete with their saddles and bridles.

Over the next few weeks, Anne bought three more ponies, and a strong, quiet cob.

"The cob will be able to take over from Bracken as a beginners' horse," she told Katy. "Bracken will be too busy getting into training for some serious show jumping. By the way, I have re-registered him in his new name, and made you and me both members so that either of us can jump him."

"Thank you, Anne," said Katy, "that's wonderful—but I should be much too scared to ride him at big shows!"

"Nonsense," Anne replied. "By the time you have helped me to get him trained for the County Show you will know as much as I do about show jumping. I am going to be very busy in the next few months—I wonder if your parents would consider letting you come to work for me during the summer holidays? It would give you a chance to make up your mind whether you really do want to work for me when you leave school."

"What a marvellous idea!" cried Katy. "I already *have* made up my mind, of course, but I'd love to work here during the holidays."

Katy's parents were quite willing to agree to the arrangement, so from the very first day of the holidays, Katy set off for the stables every morning at half past seven. It was hard work. There were so many horses to be looked after now, and so many new riders coming for lessons.

"Come down to the jumping paddock and see how Bracken is jumping now," Anne said to her one morning.

"But I've got all this tack to clean," Katy protested.

"Never mind that just now, I'll help you with it later. Major Drake has kindly offered to lend me his spring-tree saddle for the County Show, and I am going to try Bracken in it now," said Anne. "Thank goodness we got it back in time."

"Yes, and all your other saddles and bridles. They came back just in time to save you buying more for the new ponies," said Katy. "Have the thieves been sent to prison?"

"Yes," Anne replied, leading the way to the paddock, "and Snowy Peters got the longest sentence of all, because he was head of the gang. Now, I will take Bracken right round the course. Will you please put the gate at four-foot six? While you are doing that I will just take him over the cavalletti to loosen him up."

Bracken really seemed to enjoy his jumping now. He was no longer afraid of being thrashed, and he pricked his ears and went up to each jump with never the slightest attempt at a refusal. He stood well back, and with a thrust of his strong hind legs he would sail over the most formidable-looking obstacles.

"He's marvellous!" Katy exclaimed. "It will take a good horse to beat him at the County Show."

"I hope you're right," Anne smiled. "I won't jump him any more today. The show is next Saturday and I don't want him to get bored with jumping before then. I shall only give him half an hour jumping practice each day this week and I think I will take him for some nice country rides, to break the monotony for him."

"Do you think he would still run away if he got loose?" Katy asked. "He seems to trust us now."

"I wonder!" said Anne. "I don't think I will take any chances with him. Horses are funny—once they have developed a habit it is hard to break them of it. He probably used to run away because he was frightened, now he continues to do it without knowing why. Time to get back to the cleaning, now—we have six pupils coming in an hour's time."

So the day of the show drew nearer and nearer.

"I wonder if you would mind sleeping here the night before and the night after the show?" Anne asked Katy.

"I should love to!" Katy replied. "Then I can help you to get ready early in the morning, and help you again when you get back late at night."

"Exactly!" said Anne. "I should be most grateful. I have cancelled all the rides for that day, so you will only have to muck-out, feed, and generally keep an eye on the horses."

"I can manage that all right," Katy said. "I shall enjoy having the stables to myself."

"I hope you won't be lonely. I doubt if you will see anyone all day long, as most people are coming to the show," Anne said. "I'm sorry you can't come, Katy, but we couldn't leave the horses alone all that time."

"Don't you worry," Katy replied. "I should love to see you jump, of course, but looking after the horses is my job."

So Katy slept at Danepark Stables the night before the County Show. Anne put her in a neat little room with pictures of horses hung all round the walls. They got up at six o'clock next morning and began preparing Bracken for the show. He had to be fed very early to make sure he had time to digest his food before he jumped. At nine o'clock Major and Mrs. Drake arrived, and the Major helped Anne to load Bracken into the trailer. Anne, looking very smart in black jacket and boots, jumped into the Land-Rover and waved good-bye to Katy. Major and Mrs. Drake followed on in their own car.

Anne had to admit to herself, as she drove into the showground, that she was feeling rather nervous. She had jumped at many shows before, but never on such a good horse as Bracken. She was anxious not to let him down. However, she hadn't time to worry about it, once she had taken Bracken out of his trailer. Many people came up to talk to her. All her friends, pupils and their parents, wished her the best of luck.

She rode Bracken quietly round and took him over the practice jump. She saw several famous show jumpers and knew the competition was going to be very keen.

The junior jumping began, and Anne never ceased to be amazed at the sight of small ponies clearing such enormous jumps.

Soon it was time for her own event. She watched the other competitors going into the ring, one by one, until at last her own turn came.

"Come on, Bracken old boy," she said. "Let's show 'em what we can do."

Katy had enjoyed her day, alone in charge of the stables. She had groomed, fed, watered and bedded-down the stabled horses, swept the yard, tidied the tack-room and even scrubbed the floor in Anne's office.

She had been wondering all day how Anne and Bracken had fared at the show. It was late evening now, so she guessed Anne had got through into the jump-off, as she would surely have been home earlier otherwise.

Bracken's box was all ready for him. Katy had given him an extra deep bed and had mixed his feed in readiness for his return. There was nothing more to do, so she went indoors to wash and tidy herself up. She did not hear the Land-Rover drive into the yard. The first thing she heard was Anne's voice calling:

"Katy! Katy, where are you? Come quickly."

Katy ran out of the bedroom and down the stairs.

"Here I am, Anne," she called. "What's wrong? Did you win?"

Anne was standing in the doorway, her face as white as a ghost.

"Yes, yes, I won," she replied, "but never mind about that now. Bracken has fallen down in the trailer and can't get up. I don't know what to do."

Katy ran out to the yard with her. The Land-Rover and trailer stood outside Bracken's stable. The ramp was down, and, looking inside, Katy saw the big horse lying on his side, wedged between the side of the trailer and the partition.

"We shall have to take the partition out," said Anne. "It's very heavy—do you think you can help me?"

"Of course," Katy replied.

They both hurried up the ramp into the empty half of the trailer and began to unbolt the partition.

"How did it happen?" Katy asked.

"It must have been when I swerved," Anne explained. "Some idiot stopped suddenly in front of me and I had to swerve to miss him. I heard a crash behind me, but I couldn't stop to look as I was in a stream of traffic. It must have been poor old Bracken falling that I heard."

With great difficulty they dragged the partition out of the trailer. Bracken gave a grunting sigh as he found himself with room to move his legs at last. The two girls went back into the trailer to get him up. Katy reached him first and gave a little scream.

"Anne!" she cried. "His leg is covered with blood."

Anne knelt beside her horse. "Bracken! Bracken, what have you done, old boy? Quick, Katy, fetch me a sponge and some water. We won't try to get him up until I have wiped the blood away and can see how bad the cut is."

While Katy was gone, Anne stroked Bracken's neck and kept him calm by talking to him, but she could see he was bleeding badly and she was very worried. Katy was soon back and Anne began gently to sponge the wound.

"It's his knee," she said. "It's very nasty. We shall have to get the vet. We can't try to get him up—he would make it worse by struggling."

"How can he have cut it so badly?" Katy asked. "The sides of the trailer are all padded."

"I think he must have done it with his other hoof," said Anne. "Now—please go and telephone the vet. I don't want to leave him in case he tries to get up."

So Anne knelt in the straw beside Bracken and he seemed to know she would help him. Had he, Anne wondered, learned to trust her at last?

CHAPTER TWELVE

BRACKEN'S FALL

M R. BYGRAVES, the vet, was a sympathetic man who loved horses, so he understood quite well how worried Anne was.

"It's a nasty thing to happen," he told her, "but don't worry too much—I'll do what I can."

He gave Bracken an injection and dressed his knee. "I can't promise you he will ever be much good on this leg again," he said. "We still have the problem of getting the poor animal out of the trailer and into his stable. I hate to say this to you, Anne, but it might be kinder to put him out of his misery here and now."

Katy said, "Oh, no!" and began to cry, but Anne kept perfectly calm and answered quietly, "No, we'll save him if we can."

"Well, I don't know how we can get him out," said Mr. Bygraves. "He'll make that knee worse if he struggles to get up, and I doubt if the leg will support him at the moment."

"Couldn't we leave him in here," Anne suggested, "until he is able to stand?"

"The space is too cramped," Mr. Bygraves

replied, "he would be much better in a roomy stable."

"I have an idea," said Katy. "If we get a sort of sling round his stomach and pull, we could drag him out on his side. Anne could back the trailer right up to the stable door and we could pull him straight in."

"He'd be terribly heavy to move," Anne said, "and he'd be sure to struggle."

"I could give him another injection which would keep him quiet," said Mr. Bygraves, "but it would take more than the three of us to move such a big horse."

"I'll get some help," cried Anne. "Katy, find some rugs and blankets and tie them together into a long rope. I'll telephone Major Drake and David Dixon and ask them to come. Hurry!"

The Major and David came at once. Katy had fixed together all the old blankets she could lay hands on. Mr. Bygraves gave Bracken an injection which made him quite sleepy, and Anne backed the trailer right up to the open stable door.

They set about the difficult task of getting the blanket sling around Bracken's middle. Anne had slipped off his halter now that he was doped, and between them they managed to push and pull him round until he had his back towards the ramp.

It was a slow and heart-breaking job. Anne could have wept to see the great, strong animal, that only a few hours before had carried her so gallantly to victory, looking so undignified and helpless.

They all strained and heaved and struggled, pulling on the blankets with all their strength. At last the still, brown body was at the top of the ramp.

"He'll slide down on top of us all," said Major Drake. "We must put some sort of wedge to hold him, so that we can ease him down gently."

"Bales of straw," David suggested. "Stack bales of straw up against the ramp and take them away gradually as he comes down."

"A good idea," Major Drake agreed. So Katy, David and Anne fetched bales while the Major and the vet stayed with Bracken.

"Right then," said Mr. Bygraves, when the bales were built up in place, "now stand by, everyone. Gently does it."

"Thank goodness it's not a steep ramp!" said Anne.

They all pulled steadily until Bracken had slid down the first few yards of the ramp and was resting against the bales. Then David pulled away several bales and he slid down the next few yards. So they went on, until, with a final mighty effort from all of them, he was safely in his stable at last.

Katy burst into tears of relief, and Anne was surprised to find herself trembling.

"Would you like me to go and make a nice cup of tea for everyone?" David suggested to Anne.

"Thank you, David. That's a marvellous idea," Anne replied gratefully.

They pulled the blankets away from underneath Bracken and left him as comfortable as possible to wait until the effects of the drug had worn off.

Sitting in the office, sipping hot tea, Anne told the others how the accident had happened.

"What an awful thing to happen to him," David remarked. "He jumped so wonderfully at the show today. I thought it was marvellous, the way he came back into show jumping, after being forgotten about for so long, and could still beat all those other good horses."

"He may never jump again," said Anne sadly; "Mr. Bygraves can't be sure that leg will ever be really sound."

"I will do everything in my power," Mr. Bygraves promised. "We must just hope that he hasn't chipped his knee-cap. He must not move about more than you can possibly help tonight. Tomorrow, when the cut is dry, I should be able to feel if the bone is all right, or if there is any doubt, we can send him for an X-ray. Anyway, I should watch him tonight to see that he keeps as still as possible. He's not likely to put any weight on that leg—it will be too painful. If he does stand on it, we can be pretty sure it is not too bad after all."

Major Drake, David, and the vet all said good night and went home.

"I shall sleep in Bracken's stable tonight," Anne said. "I'm not going to take my eyes off him."

"Then I shall sleep there, too!" Katy declared. "We can take it in turns to sleep and to watch him."

"That's very good of you, Katy," Anne said. "I must admit I should be very grateful for your company."

So they fetched blankets and pillows and made themselves as comfortable as possible in the straw. Bracken raised his head once or twice to look at them, but otherwise lay still.

"I'm so glad he's not struggling and trying to stand up," said Anne. "He might start his leg bleeding again if he moves."

"He's a wonderful horse," Katy remarked. "I'm sure he knows we are here to help him. Do tell me how he jumped at the show."

"He was really marvellous!" Anne said. "When we first jumped he seemed a bit lazy, but in the jump-off he woke up and jumped magnificently! The commentator had found out all about him, because he announced, 'This horse has been out of show jumping for a year or two. He used to be known as Caramel and had a promising future. He is now making a come-back with a new rider, under the name of Bracken.' When we won, everyone cheered like mad. Oh, yes—I won a huge silver cup and twenty-five pounds! I have left the cup in the Land-Rover—I forgot all about it, with Bracken's accident."

So they talked, until Katy dozed off. Eventually, Anne began to nod, so she had to wake Katy and ask her to keep watch. All night long they took turns at watching the injured horse, and all night long he hardly moved.

It was Katy's turn to watch when dawn began to light up the sky. Anne had been soundly asleep for the last hour. Suddenly, Bracken raised his head.

"Steady, boy," Katy whispered. "Lie still."

But he stretched, rustling the deep straw. Then he put out both forelegs and, before Katy could get to him, with a mighty heave, he sprang to his feet. He stood squarely on all four feet for a moment, then, slowly and stiffly, he moved across to his water bucket.

Katy shook Anne by the shoulder. "He's up!" she hissed in Anne's ear. "He's standing up."

Anne opened two bleary eyes and peered over her blankets. "Is he all right?" she asked.

"He got up quite easily," Katy replied. "He can't walk much, but I don't think there can be any bones broken."

Anne was so pleased, she got up and went quietly across to Bracken. She buried her face in his coarse, black mane and whispered:

"You're going to be all right, old boy. I know you are!"

CHAPTER THIRTEEN

A TURN FOR THE BETTER

BRACKEN's leg healed slowly. He had to be kept in the stable for three weeks to rest it, and then Mr. Bygraves said he must be turned out to grass for two months.

"It will be some time before he can be ridden again," he warned Anne.

"I don't mind about that, as long as he gets well," Anne replied. "I just wonder whether we shall ever be able to catch him again, once he is turned loose!"

"He seems to be very fond of you," the vet remarked. "I should think you will catch him easily."

"You have never seen us trying to catch him," Anne laughed. "It's almost impossible."

However, it was quite true that Bracken seemed to have grown very fond of Anne while she had nursed his injured leg.

"I just hope you don't forget me when you have your freedom," she said to the horse, as she patted his neck and turned him loose in the big field. Bracken snuffled at her pockets and did not seem to realize for a moment that he was free. Then he suddenly squealed with joy, and trotted off, with a very noticeable limp, to enjoy the fresh grass. Anne threw his halter over her shoulder and went back to the yard.

Danepark Stables was doing well and Anne was beginning to think about having an Indoor School erected before the winter. Katy would be going back to school at the end of the summer, but her mind was quite made up, and when she left school next year Anne would be pleased to employ her, and to begin her training as an Assistant Instructress. It seemed to Anne that all her dearest wishes were coming true. All she wanted now was for Bracken to get well and be able to jump again.

She mounted Zulu and took her pupils down to the paddock for their lesson.

Katy was thoroughly enjoying her working holiday. Her parents had wanted to take her to the seaside for a week, but Katy refused to go.

"I'd much rather work at the stables," she declared. "And besides, how would Anne manage without me? She is so busy now during the school holidays. There are masses of children wanting to ride. Every day we are rushed off our feet. Anne is so busy giving lessons that she has to leave nearly all the other work to me."

Her mother gave a sigh of resignation. "Well, Katy, it seems you are content to spend the rest of your life mucking-out stables and cleaning tack."

"Of course not," Katy replied. "I'm going to be an Instructress. When I leave school and work for Anne all the time, she will train me so that I can take the examination and be properly qualified. I *wish* I didn't have to go back to school!"

"Well, you do," said her mother. "You have another year to go before you can leave. In the meantime I will go and talk to Anne about your future career. If your heart is set on working with horses, your father and I will not stand in your way."

Katy kissed her mother gratefully and set off for the stables.

The holidays, which, at the beginning, had seemed to stretch endlessly before her, were now drawing all too quickly to a close. There was a feeling of autumn in the air. The mornings were misty, and in the evenings darkness fell quickly.

"Isn't it sad?" Katy said to Anne. "I hate to see the leaves turning brown and to realize that summer is over."

"I think autumn is very beautiful," Anne replied. "There is a lot to be said for winter, too. I love sharp, frosty mornings and the ponies in their thick, fluffy coats."

"Do you think I could come and work for you in the Christmas holidays, too?" Katy asked.

"I should be very pleased if you really want to," Anne said. "I can manage on my own during term-time, but there is such a lot to do when the children are on holiday."

So Katy went unwillingly back to school, hoping the term would not seem too long. It was the worst term of the year, Katy thought, as it was too dark after school to go to the stables. She did her best to concentrate on her schoolwork, and spent her evenings struggling with homework. There were always the week-ends to look forward to.

At the end of November came the time for Anne to catch Bracken and see if his leg was sound again. She had been visiting him every day, of course, to feed him, but had not, as yet, tried to halter him. She filled her pockets with oats and threw his halter over her shoulder. When she reached the gate she could see him grazing in the far corner. She climbed on to the gate and whistled to him.

"Bracken!" she called. "Bracken, here, old boy!"

The horse gave a whinny of recognition and began to walk slowly towards her. He tossed his head and broke into a trot. In a moment he had pressed his warm muzzle into her hand.

"Bracken, you dear old boy, you're really pleased to see me," said Anne, "and you didn't limp one little bit!"

He stood quite still while Anne put on his halter. She led him happily back to his stable. It seemed that Bracken had at last forgotten his unhappy past and knew he had a friend he could trust.

Anne took him into his stable and brushed him well. Then she telephoned the vet to come and look at him and see whether he would soon be fit for work again.

Mr. Bygraves was much pleased with Bracken's recovery.

"He seems to be perfectly sound on that leg now," he remarked. "I should start him with some light work—just walking exercise for the first week, and gradually increase the work if he seems all right. If there is any sign of lameness in that leg, send for me at once."

Bracken was full of high spirits after his long rest and Anne found it difficult to keep him walking. Each day she rode him up the lane and round the village and she had to keep saying:

"Steady, Bracken, steady. You must walk," as he tried to break into a trot.

The second week she gave him several short, slow trots and the third week was able to begin schooling him in the paddock.

"Bracken is really lively now," she told Katy one Saturday morning. "He is as sound as a bell and I intend to start jumping him again. I want to have him really fit, ready for the show jumping next season."

"He certainly looks very well now," Katy agreed.

"It will be exciting if you take him to the big shows."

Bracken was obviously glad to be jumping again. Every day Anne took him over two or three jumps, and at week-ends Katy jumped him.

The builders had started work, erecting the Indoor School, and Anne hoped it would be finished in time for the Christmas holidays, because then the children would be able to ride whatever the weather.

"It's going to be marvellous, having an Indoor School!" said Katy, as she and Anne watched the men fixing the roof. "We shall be able to ride on winter evenings when it's dark outside, and when it rains or snows we can still have lessons in here."

"We can have little jumping competitions in here during the Christmas holidays," Anne said. "That is, if it's finished in time. Do you think it will be?" she asked the foreman, who was standing nearby.

"It will be finished in another couple of days now, except for the painting," he answered.

Anne was much pleased to hear this. For one thing, it meant Bracken's training could continue when the ground was unfit for jumping in the paddock.

The builders kept their promise, and when the children came to ride in the Christmas holidays, they were all excited at having their riding lessons indoors. Many more grown-ups came to ride too, now that they could ride on winter evenings.

Katy and Anne were kept very busy, but they always found time between them to give Bracken his jumping practice. Katy loved to have the chance to jump him when Anne was too busy.

So Danepark Stables grew steadily prosperous, and Bracken prepared for his return to show jumping.

CHAPTER FOURTEEN

THE BIG SHOW

"IT seemed such a long time ahead when I made the entry," said Anne. She and Katy were sitting in her office studying a Horse Show schedule. "Now it's almost on top of us—next week, in fact."

"It's the biggest show for miles around, isn't it?" asked Katy.

"Yes," Anne replied. "I wish we could have gone to some small shows first, but we've been so busy. The winter was over so soon, this year—it must have been because the weather did not worry us, as we could ride under cover. Anyway, this is one of the first big shows of the season. Who knows? If we win here, we might end up at the Horse of the Year Show."

"That would be terrific!" said Katy. "But don't be too ambitious."

"I'm only joking," laughed Anne. "I wouldn't have time to take up show jumping as seriously as that. I really never should have started it at all, but with Bracken falling into our hands by accident, as it were, it seemed a shame to waste his talent.

I shall want you to come to this show with me, Katy. I couldn't manage on my own."

"I was hoping you'd ask me," Katy smiled. "But what about the other horses?"

"The show is on a Saturday, and I shall have to cancel all the riding lessons; but I'm sure Heather and Clive will come and feed the horses for me," Anne said.

It was a long journey to the show. They loaded Bracken into the trailer, and stowed his saddle, bridle, brushes, and Anne's white breeches, black jacket and boots into the back of the Land-Rover.

"It's too far to drive on a hot day, in boots and breeches," said Anne. She wore old jeans and some comfortable sandals. "I can change in the trailer when we get there," she said.

It was a big Horse Show, to which riders came from all over the country. There were some magnificent horse-boxes parked all around, and smartly-dressed riders and their grooms were leading the horses down the ramps.

"There are some famous horses and riders here today," Anne remarked, as she steered the Land-Rover into a quiet corner and parked it. She opened the door and sprang out. Katy heard her give a little cry of pain, and hurried round to see what was wrong.

Anne was sitting on the ground nursing her ankle. "Oh, I've twisted my ankle," she groaned.

"There was a pot-hole in the ground just where I landed. It's terribly painful—I hope I haven't broken it."

"Take off your sock and let me look," said Katy.

Anne obeyed. "Goodness," she exclaimed, "look how swollen it is."

"You stay where you are, and I will go and fetch someone from the First Aid post," Katy said.

"No, no," Anne replied. "I'm sure I can walk there if you help me. I don't want them carting me off on a stretcher, thank you. Bend down and let me put my arm round your shoulders. If you can lift me up I'm certain I can hop there."

"You really shouldn't," Katy protested. "If your ankle is broken, you could do it a lot of damage. Let me at least get one of the First Aid people to look at it before you try to stand. Here, I'll prop you up against the Land-Rover so that you are more comfortable."

Anne was in too much pain to argue. Katy dragged her into a more convenient position, and left her.

"Could you tell me where the First Aid post is, please?" Katy asked the first person she met.

"Sorry, dear, I haven't seen it."

Katy ran on towards the main ring. At last she saw a small tent marked First Aid. Several men and women in uniform were standing inside.

"Can you come quickly, please?" she pleaded. "My friend has hurt her ankle and can't walk."

"Show us where she is." Two men picked up a stretcher and followed Katy through the crowds.

Anne was very glad to see Katy return. Her ankle had turned black and blue. One of the men examined it carefully and pronounced it to be badly sprained.

"Don't worry, it's not broken," he assured her. "You must not walk on it, though. We'll take you back to the First Aid post on the stretcher and treat it for you, but you will not have to put any weight on it for a few days."

They rolled Anne on to the stretcher, and Katy followed them back to the tent and waited while Anne's ankle was treated. As she waited, she had time to think, and suddenly she thought of Bracken. She wondered how they would get home again, if Anne could not drive. Just then, a nurse came out and said: "Are you Katy?" Katy nodded. "Well, the young lady would like to see you," said the nurse.

Katy went into the tent. Anne sat there, looking rather pale, her ankle strapped up with bandages.

"Katy," she said, "do you think you could take Bracken in this jumping competition? It would be a shame for him not to jump, now we are here. You get on very well, jumping at home, and I know you could do it."

Katy was stunned. At last she said, "I'd love to, Anne. I'll do my very best for you."

"I know you will. Now, you must go to the secretary and explain that we are substituting the rider. You can wear my clothes; we are much the same size, so they should fit you. I only wish I could help you to get Bracken out of the trailer and tacked up. Do you think you can manage?"

"Of course I can," Katy declared.

"Well, off you go then," said Anne, "and good luck. I shall be watching—they are going to put me in a deck-chair at the ring-side."

Katy hurried off to find the secretary. There was so much to be done, there was no time to feel nervous or worried.

When she had arranged these things with the secretary, she went back to the Land-Rover and found Anne's riding kit. She opened the groom's door of the trailer and went into the empty half to change.

Looking in at Bracken, she said, "Well, Bracken, you've only got me, instead of Anne. Please be very good, and I'll try to remember all Anne has taught me about jumping you."

Bracken snorted and stamped his foot and Katy guessed he was tired of being left in the trailer. She hurriedly peeled off her sweater and skirt and began to dress in Anne's beautiful white breeches and white shirt. She pulled on the long, black boots. They were rather large, but quite comfortable once she had fastened the straps round her legs. The black jacket was a good fit, and the hat was just right, too. When she stepped out of the trailer again, she felt she looked like a professional show jumper, and this helped to give her confidence.

Next she had the difficult task of letting down the ramp single-handed. She had helped Anne to do it many times, but it was easy then, with one on each side. She looked round desperately, to see if there was anyone she could ask for help, but there was no one she knew.

She reached up to slip out the securing pin on the left, when a voice behind her said:

"Can I help?"

She turned gratefully, and saw Mr. Stringer behind her.

"Oh, that's very kind of you," said Katy. "It is rather difficult for me, as the ramp is heavy."

"You're looking very smart today," Mr. Stringer remarked. "Are you taking that horse in the Novice class again?"

"Oh, no," Katy replied. "You were quite right about him. He *was* Snowy Peters' horse. We didn't mean to cheat, you know, that day at Bedloe. We didn't know where he came from."

"That's all past and forgotten now," said Mr.

Stringer. "Just as long as you're not competing against my son again today."

He helped Katy to lower the ramp, and watched as she led Bracken out.

"I'd know that horse anywhere. I knew I wasn't wrong about him," Mr. Stringer said. "I hear Snowy has gone to gaol, for stealing tack. He always was a bad 'un. I packed up working for him because I couldn't stand the way he treated his horses."

Katy saddled and bridled Bracken and mounted him.

"I see the horse has lost his nervousness," observed Mr. Stringer. "Can you catch him all right now?"

"Yes," Katy replied, "I believe he has grown quite fond of Anne and me."

"Well, good luck. I shall be watching you jump. He used to jump through fear. Snowy used to thrash him if he ever touched a jump, and if he ever refused—well! So I shall be interested to see how he goes for you today." Mr. Stringer watched Katy ride away.

Katy rode Bracken quietly round the showground to settle him down. He seemed unusually lively, and keen to go. Perhaps it was being back at a big show again, after so long, Katy thought.

She took him to the practice jump, and he sprang over it like a stag. He pranced and cavorted, and behaved quite unlike the beginners' horse which he used to be. Katy began to wonder if she would be able to manage him when she got in the ring.

It was time for the riders to walk over the course and look at the jumps. Most of them had grooms to hold their horses while they went, but Katy did not know what to do with Bracken, until a small boy appeared at her side and asked, "Can I hold your horse for you, miss?" Katy gratefully handed him the reins.

The riders were walking round in small groups, and Katy was pleased when a young woman fell into step beside her and began to chat.

"Don't like the look of that wall," she said, and Katy agreed that neither did she.

"We'd better pace out the double," said the young woman. Katy was glad to have someone to give her advice.

The jumps seemed to tower above Katy's head. She hoped they would not look so terrifying from Bracken's back.

"There's a sharp turn here into the parallel poles," her companion remarked. "Come into it steady or you'll not be collected enough to take off right. Now, I think we've had a good look at everything. Don't take the wrong course, whatever you do. Better go and get mounted. Good luck."

"Thanks," said Katy, "same to you. Thank you for your help."

Katy went off to find Bracken.

The small boy was still standing where Katy had left him, in tears. There was no sign of Bracken.

"Where's my horse?" Katy shrieked at the boy. "What have you done with him?"

The boy sniffed loudly: "Weren't my fault," he sobbed, "I just went to flick some flies off his head with my stick and he reared right up and ran off. There's some men chasing him now—look, over there!"

Katy looked where he was pointing. Bracken was way over in a far corner of the showground, with four or five men running after him.

"They'll frighten him," she cried. "They'll never catch him like that. Oh, what am I to do?" She burst into tears.

It was useless to stand around weeping, however, and Katy quickly realized this. She ran across the field, hoping at least to persuade the men to stop chasing Bracken.

"Katy, Katy, where are you going?" It was Anne's voice from the crowd round the ringside.

Katy pushed through the spectators and found Anne, sitting in a deck-chair with her foot propped up on a box.

"Oh, Anne," Katy wept, "it's Bracken. I left a boy holding him—I forgot he might still be nervous of strangers. He's run away, and some men are chasing him all over the place. What a terrible day this is!"

Anne clapped a hand to her forehead. "Crikey!" she exclaimed. "I heard there was a horse loose, but I didn't know it was Bracken. Go and tell them to stop chasing him, as fast as you can. If I can get over there I think he'll still come to me."

"But how can you get there?" Katy asked. "You mustn't walk!"

"Don't waste time arguing," Anne said. "Leave it to me. But go quickly, please!"

So Katy ran, stumbling over tussocks of grass in the big, black boots. Her feet felt like lead and her legs like rubber, but she forced herself on. She could see Bracken galloping round, and the men running and waving their arms. As soon as she was within shouting distance she stopped running and tried to call out, but she could only gasp breathlessly. She stood, panting, for a second, then, cupping her hands to her mouth she managed to shout: "Stop!" One of the men turned to look at her. "Leave him, please," she called.

The man stopped running and shouted to his friends: "Hi, this young lady wants you."

They all stood still, and waited for Katy to come nearer.

"Please don't chase him," she begged. "He's so frightened of you, he'll just keep running away. Leave him to me."

"Well, miss, if you can catch him, you're a marvel," one of the men laughed.

"I don't suppose I can," Katy replied. "If we leave him to settle down, he may start to graze and forget his fright. I'm very grateful to you for trying to help, but you see, he was badly treated by a man he used to belong to, so he's easily scared. It's useless to run after him."

"All right, miss, we understand," said the man. "Anyway, it's given us some exercise! Come on, mates, I don't know about the rest of you but all that running has made me thirsty."

They walked away, laughing.

As Katy had hoped, when he found he was no longer pursued, Bracken stood still and began to graze. Katy flopped down on the grass and wondered what to do next.

A moment later, she heard an engine, and turning to look, she saw a car coming towards her. The driver was a stranger, but seated next to him was Anne. Katy ran to meet them.

"He's grazing quietly now," she said. "Do you think we can catch him?"

"I certainly hope so," Anne replied. "By the way, Katy, this is Mr. Redman. I'm afraid I press-ganged him into helping me."

Mr. Redman laughed. "Not at all," he said, "I'm always glad of the chance to rescue damsels in distress. Now, can I help to capture the runaway?

I've had strict orders from the First Aid tent that I mustn't let you walk on that leg."

"I know, and it makes things very awkward," Anne complained. "I had hoped to hobble across to Bracken, but as you won't allow me to, I shall just have to hope he'll come to me."

"I don't think he'll come when you are in a car, and with someone he doesn't know," Katy said.

"I'm afraid you're right, Katy. Do you think you and Mr. Redman between you could carry me across to that old tree stump? If I sit on that and call him, he may come to me; then you, Katy, can come and take him when I have hold of his bridle. Mr. Redman can drive the car over and help me back in."

It seemed the only solution, so with Anne's arms round each of their shoulders, Katy and Mr. Redman helped her to hop across to the tree stump. Then they drove away some distance, so that there was no danger of Bracken taking fright at the sight of the car.

Anne sat silently on the stump for some time, watching Bracken graze. Sometimes he moved a little nearer, and sometimes further away. At last she called to him, quietly. He raised his head and looked towards her.

"Bracken, here boy," she called, a little louder this time.

His reins were over his head, trailing on the

ground. He trod on them once, as he walked slowly towards her. It made him hesitate for a moment.

"Good boy, come along, Bracken," Anne called soothingly.

Bracken began to walk on again, and in a moment was snuffling affectionately into Anne's hand. Slowly, gently, she took hold of the reins. She patted his neck and spoke quietly to him, while she waited for Katy to walk across from the car.

"Here we are, Katy," she said, handing her the reins. "Here is your mount, safe and sound. Now, go in and win."

Katy mounted cautiously, then rode away, leaving Mr. Redman to assist Anne back into the car.

It was almost time now for her event to start. Bracken seemed none the worse for his escapade, and pricked his ears at the sight of the jumps as they neared the ring.

"Well, Bracken," said Katy, "it really doesn't seem to be our day, but let's see what we can do."

CHAPTER FIFTEEN

RIDING HIGH

KATY'S turn to go into the ring came much sooner than she had expected. The jumps looked slightly less terrifying with Bracken's solid form beneath her, but they were still enormous.

Bracken bounded into the ring and it took all Katy's strength to control him and make him circle collectedly before the bell rang. The big horse seemed to know the meaning of the bell and, with no signal from Katy, he turned and thundered towards the first jump. It was a low brush and he cleared it with little effort and made for the next. The second jump was a crossed poles and they sailed over. Katy knew she was merely a passenger, and all she had to do was to stay on his back and steer him over the right course.

Next came a hog's back, and then a big spread. After the white gate came the sharp turn into the parallel poles and Katy knew she must steady him here. She put all her weight against him and gave a mighty tug on the reins. It brought Bracken back on to his hocks, but one of his hind feet slipped and he almost came down. He recovered miraculously, but before Katy could regain her balance he had leaped the parallel poles. Katy found herself clinging desperately to his mane. As he landed she lost both stirrups and almost fell off over his shoulder. Bracken steadied long enough for Katy to heave herself back into the saddle, but she was still groping for her stirrups as he set off for the triple. She thrust her feet hard home into the irons just as he collected himself for the first part, some red and white poles. He changed legs cleverly and cleared the Road Closed, which was in the centre, and Katy thought, with horror, that they had tipped the white gate which was the last part, but it did not fall.

Katy began to feel a little more secure, and less helpless. Bracken's pace had steadied somewhat and he was behaving more like his usual self. The dragon's teeth presented no problems, neither did the rustic poles, but, looming ever closer, Katy could see the formidable wall. It was huge and solid-looking. Katy would have fled from it in terror, but she knew Bracken had sufficient courage for both of them, so she took hold of his mane and prepared for the take-off.

"Come on, Bracken," Katy gasped between clenched teeth.

She felt the thrust of his powerful quarters, felt the rush of air in her face, and then they were safely over. They put the last jump behind them and cantered out of the ring to the sound of thunderous applause.

Katy felt weak. Her legs seemed to fold beneath her as she dismounted. People clustered about her saying, "Well done, well done."

The young woman who had walked the course with her rode up. "Some horse you've got there!" she remarked. "He went like a bomb. I thought you'd had it when he slipped, though. Almost came off, didn't you?"

"Very nearly," Katy admitted.

"You'll have to watch out for that turn in the jump-off," the young woman continued. "It's against the clock, and he may slip again when he turns at speed. Have you got studs in his shoes?"

"Goodness, I forgot about the studs!" Katy exclaimed. Anne had them in the pocket of her jeans, but so much had happened since they arrived at the show that they had been quite overlooked. "Shall I have time to go and put them in now?" Katy asked.

"Oh, yes," her new-found friend replied. "There are still several more waiting to jump."

So Katy remounted and rode off to find Anne.

Anne was surprised to see her. "Katy, you still have to jump again," she said. "What are you doing here?"

"The studs," Katy gasped. "You've still got the studs in your pocket."

"Oh, I'm so sorry, Katy. How stupid of me to forget them! No wonder Bracken slipped. That was a fantastic round you jumped. My heart was in my mouth from beginning to end. You really hung on by the skin of your teeth!"

"I know. I was terrified," said Katy. "Bracken seemed to become a different horse as soon as he went into the ring. There was nothing for me to do but cling on."

"Well, don't interfere with him this time," Anne advised her. "He seems to do very well without anyone's assistance, and you might slow him down. The way he went just now, he should do very well against the clock."

Katy screwed the studs into the specially made holes in Bracken's shoes and mounted him again.

"Don't worry, Katy," Anne said. "You'll be all right."

"Oddly enough," Katy replied, "I'm rather looking forward to it this time."

She rode slowly back to the collecting ring, hoping to appear calm and unflustered. She walked Bracken up and down while she waited, to keep him warm and relaxed.

There were six to jump-off, and Katy was drawn last. The clear round she had to beat was in a time of fifty-nine seconds. It seemed impossible to beat, but Katy felt she could be very lucky and come second or third.

The bell rang and they were off. Katy urged Bracken on. "Come on, Bracken! Let's show 'em how to do it."

Bracken pricked his ears and flew the brush. Katy let him take the jumps at his own speed, only steadying him slightly on the turns. It was like being astride an express train. He snorted and blew and the sweat lathered his neck. He seemed to sense the urgency, and Katy could tell that Bracken knew the game well. He may have learned to jump from fear of Snowy Peters, but he was thoroughly enjoying it now.

They rattled the rustic poles, and then came the wall, higher than ever now. Katy could not see over it. Bracken gave a mighty spring and then it was safely behind them. One more jump to go, and the crowd was gasping with excitement.

The clock said fifty-six seconds as they passed the finish at a flat-out gallop. The crowd roared, and somehow Katy regained control of Bracken in time to make a triumphant exit from the ring.

Anne could hardly keep herself from jumping out of the chair to meet Katy and Bracken as they rode back towards her. Bracken stepped proudly, the huge, double, red-and-white rosette making his head look almost handsome. Who would dare now to say he had a Roman nose, or was ugly in any way?

He dropped his head and snuffled at Anne's pocket and she produced a sugar lump for him.

"You were marvellous, Katy," said Anne.

"No, I wasn't. I was terrible," Katy protested.

"He did it all himself, you know. I just showed him which way to go. He's a darling. How is your ankle, Anne? I mean, you can't drive home, can you?"

"I've got it all arranged," Anne replied. "Mr. Redman has kindly offered to drive us home, and his wife will follow on with their car. Fortunately they live quite near us. Now you must go and put Bracken in the trailer. Put his rug on so that he doesn't catch a chill, and then we can go home."

When at last Bracken was back in his own stable, contentedly tucking in to a good feed, and Katy had fed and watered the other horses, she went in to sit beside Anne who lay on a settee.

"Heather and Clive seem to have coped very well," she said. "The horses are all fine."

"Good," said Anne. "It's been quite a day. I'm very proud of you, Katy, and as for Bracken—he need never fear falling into bad hands again. He has a home here for the rest of his life. I wouldn't sell him for a fortune."

"No," said Katy, "he's a horse in a million. Now I simply must go home, if you are sure there's nothing else I can do for you. My mother will never believe me, when I tell her all that has happened today."

So Katy went home, leaving Bracken quietly dozing in his stable, the memory of her clear round vivid in her mind, never to be forgotten.